DOGWOOD AFTERNOONS

DOGWOOD AFTERNOONS

Kim Chapin

THE BODLEY HEAD
LONDON

British Library Cataloguing
in Publication Data:
Dogwood afternoons.
I. Title
813'. 54[F]   PS 3553.H 279/
ISBN 0 370 30721 6

© Kim Chapin 1985
Printed and bound in
Great Britain for
The Bodley Head Ltd,
30 Bedford Square,
London WC1B 3RP
by St Edmundsbury Press, Bury St Edmunds

*First published by Farrar, Straus and
Giroux, New York, 1985
First published in Great Britain 1986.*

FOR MY MOTHER
Roberta C. Chapin

PART ONE

CHAPTER
1

Andrew Mavis here, goddamn.

It is a nudge past eight o'clock on the morning of eighteenth April, nineteen sixty-four, a Saturday, and I am running high down the back straight of the Terminus Motor Speedway, a new track to the Circuit, two miles around and flat-bellied in the turns, narrow as streaked lightning on the straights and greasy as owl shit everywhere. I cadge a glance at the thin red tachometer needle, quivering steadily at 7250, and with an uncanny accuracy that amazes even me, I estimate my speed at one hundred and eighty-three bulldog miles an hour, give or take a tick. And do you want to know what I'm thinking? I am thinking this: Andrew, old buddy, at this precise moment there is no one else in the whole world who is moving across the face of God's fanciful earth in a racing stock car, or in anything else, quite as rapidly as you are. You are the man. You are the only one. You are dialed in to zero. This is what you were born to do and now, at the advanced age of twenty-three soon to be twenty-four, you are doing it. You are really doing it. Where is my silk scarf?

The clear-eyed sun raises one eyebrow over the third-turn guard rail and soon will flicker-blind me on each passage. No problem. From the shadows in the same turn, trickles of the morning's heavy dew slide down the slight banking. In the center of the infield there stands a grove of dogwood trees. Now, who in his right mind would build a race track so slick and flat and narrow as is this, yet plant dogwoods right where the paying customers can't see through them to the other side of the track:

What's happenin' offen number two, Grover?

Don't rightly know, Jeremiah. Cain't see fer the dogwoods.

Yet they are strangely transfixing. The lush blooms are so heavy with the early mist that the dark and gnarled boughs bend gently to the ground, puffs of melting ice cream on a stick. My balls tingle. I'm revved up, wired, strung tighter than a fiddle. I lean forward. My knees and elbows, all gangly and akimbo, embrace the padded steering wheel, wrapped with yards and yards of sticky black electrical tape. So hard do I strain against my shoulder harness and lap belt that tomorrow I know I'll have the blacks-and-blues tattooed across my chest and belly with such definition that they might as well be painted on. It happens all the time. I like my belts cinched tight. I can feel the car more; establish a oneness with the car that isn't there if I'm loose and flip-flopping around. Particularly now. Even with the belts drawn taut, my slim-hipped body slides side to side across the width of the contoured driver's seat, shaped not for me and only vaguely with me in mind.

I am a visitor here.

. . .

Last night the Peterbilt rig, eighteen wheels and forty feet long and thirteen feet high, rolled into Four Corners, seventy-two loblolly country miles north of Terminus, and blew its air brakes to a stop on the square in front of the copper-green statue of old Colonel Stokes. Wynn and I were with One-Eye chowing at Miss Dee's, and from our window booth we stared bug-eyed, at least I did, as two mechanics dressed in white—white slacks, white polo shirts, white jackets, even white shoes and shoelaces— jumped down from the high cab door and walked across the cobbled square and through the door of the small cafe. They nodded to One-Eye, not knowing Wynn or me from the off ox.

You fellows lost? asked One-Eye, knowing that Four Corners was not the most direct route to Terminus from anywhere.

Miss Dee still serve steaks and tamales? asked the taller of the two. His nonchalance barely stayed the civil side of arrogance. His nose was bent, my guess was by a tire iron.

Assured that she did, the shorter of the two, his face and neck a prickly red from midday racing suns, said, Then we ain't lost a'tall. We'll take our dinner here and be at Terminus in ninety minutes' time.

We wolfed our food, Wynn and I, and together hurried out into the spring night's cool fog. The transporter, like the clothing of its mechanics, was white-on-white, save for a brilliant chrome maidenhead and chrome wheels and a wide black slash on either side of the trailer that ran the diagonal from front high to back low. Inside the monster rig, we knew, were two race cars and enough spare parts for at least one weekend of racing. The cars could be rebuilt from scratch on the spot if circumstances

7

so contrived. On the cab doors, in bold and calligraphic script, were the words: Dorsen Motor Company Racing Team. And below: Team Manager Jean-Pierre Andriotti. And farther below: Drivers Clyde Warden and Dink MacIntosh. Around this last name was a fine black box. Six weeks before, Dink had flown his two-lung Apache through the roof of the state liquor store in Anarchy.

Roll them out, said One-Eye.

He and the two Dorsen mechanics had materialized silently behind us. With some reluctance, I thought, Bent Nose and Red Face complied. They lowered the tailgate of the trailer, placed a ramp of wood and steel behind, and ever so gently let out the hand winches that tethered the cars inside. And then they were there in front of us in the empty square, sleek in the light from the bright cafe and from a rising crescent moon. They were otherworldly, ghostly, and all in white save for the same black stripes on the transporter, only these stripes began at the center-front of the hood and flowed along the sides of the cars until they reached the rear quarterpanels and trailed off into the night. Their night-rider unreality was enhanced by an absence of decals or other paintings, even numbers. In Gothic script two fingers high beneath the driver's-side window on one, I read: Andrew Mavis; on the other: Wynn Tatum.

Wynn feigned a faint and fell limply backward into One-Eye's arms. I whistled low and long and walked time-lessly around both cars, shark-mean and glistening in the phantom light.

Wynn recovered himself and smiled, his bloodhound face bemused and enigmatic.

Are they equal? he asked.

As equal as we can make them, said Bent Nose. You

can work with us tomorrow, if you think it's needed, to get them where you feel they ought to be.

· · ·

I balloon-foot the accelerator at the entrance to turn three. Flame and raging gases boil through the exhaust headers. The edges of the searing heat seep through the floorboard and warm my feet, a good feeling.

One day two years ago, when I was learning how to drive and the Circuit seemed no closer than a dream, I drove forever round and round the dirt at Four Corners, seeking to find the feel of my car and doubting whether I ever would. One-Eye in the pits pinched his stopwatches and shook his head on every lap as I wrestled with my erratic charge, the fire in my brain building with each passage. I smelled smoke; I looked down at the floorboard and saw smoke. I spun the car to a dead-dime stop and bailed out to seek on hands and knees the cooling infield grass. Only then did the pain from my right heel override my anger and frustration.

You didn't feel the pain until you'd left the car? asked One-Eye with curiosity and awe. It was a broken weld. I checked.

My mind was elsewhere, I said as One-Eye lanced the glistening blister and let the juices gush. My mind was filled with thoughts of how to turn this shit-box left.

I gestured toward the car, which maintained innocence.

Now, I wear square-toed cowboy boots from Billy Winslow's General Store on the square and wrap the heel of the right with foam-rubber pads secured with asbestos tape. My left foot I can plant against a side bar of the roll cage. And though it's been two years, and more, the skin is tender still.

9

I talk to myself at speed, whether I'm scrubbing tires or racing ding-dong on a superspeedway such as this, though I've yet to do so much of that, or banzai banging in the forty-lappers on the little dirt bullrings such as that whore of a track in Four Corners, where there's slam-bam thank-you-ma'am kamikaze fun without tears every night out. Ah, Andrew, will you ever touch the dirt again? Also, for the record, I yell, scream, rant, rave, pound the steering column, scratch my balls, and make obscene gestures at the littlest old ladies I can find and also at the youngest and most stacked. I show no favoritism. If still my unbound energy offers to make bile in my guts, I sing, loudly and profanely, or mime posey words of calm and soothing. My favorite thus begins: Buffalo Bill's / defunct / who used to / ride a watersmooth-silver / stallion . . .

I slide through number four and can hear the tires screech *wheek wheeek wheek* as the car drifts to the outside rail. Where begins the front grandstand, twenty-seven thousand glistening aluminum state-of-the-art empty seats, the car grabs hold and I aim for the apex of the slight dog-leg bend on the main straight. Already I've experimented some, and if I cut the bend so that my left-side tires kick up red dust—damn narrow racing groove—I'm on the perfect line for turn one, not that far distant. A second beyond the apex, I pass the pits. The other car is there, and Wynn, a matchstick stuck between his teeth, starts to climb in through his driver's-side window. One-Eye lifts the chalkboard. 5-L, it says: five laps left. Next to One-Eye, Andriotti snaps his stopwatches. One-Eye wears coveralls and shitkickers; Andriotti sports a silk suit from Hong Kong, a tapered tailored shirt from Carnaby Street, a pair of soft-leather shoes from Italy. I've never seen his shoes dusty. I've never seen any part of Andriotti that was anything but immaculate. No wonder they called him the Watchmaker when he was racing fancy cars in Europe before the war and after. He's a nice man, I think—courteous, friendly, though not lovable.

One-Eye, now, he's different, and I don't ever mind saying I love that old man. Not so old. He looks younger than he ought to look, given all he's been through. I can't remember the last time anybody called him Mr. Rivers, or even Wendell, with the accent such that it comes out *Wen*-dell. Certainly nobody in Four Corners ever has. He has always been One-Eye.

• • •

I am the man. I am on the point and my balls tingle. I have been waiting for this moment for three months, since the day in January when we all assembled around momma's kitchen table: Wynn and his daddy, Spencer; me and my crippled daddy, Wylie, who, without his brace, used a straight-back chair as a walker to make his way to the table, his left leg dragging behind him; and One-Eye and Andriotti. A sodden winter's rain that had curled in over the gray mountains to the north, called the Quahills, played a snare-drum rhythm on the roof.

Andriotti cut to the nut right away, his lilting voice an alliance of wondrous accents, all of them Continental, some of them affected for the drama of the occasion.

I can't offer either of you a factory ride, he said, but our shop in Ashley Oaks has one position open, for what you Americans call a gofer. It's the shit work. You push brooms. You make coffee runs for the boys. You haul the race-car rigs to hell and back. The pay is a dollar twenty-five an hour and you don't punch the clock after fifty hours. I can't say more, but if there's free time you might get help on a car of your own. And if that works out . . .

He shrugged, knowing he had said enough. He could have lured Wynn and me halfway round the world with a lesser promise.

When he left, we looked to One-Eye for his wisdom.

He likes you boys, One-Eye said. He's seen what you can do up here on dirt, and unless my guess is all askew, you've both got solid futures, if not with him, then with someone else. But they didn't call him the Watchmaker for nothing, when he was driving the fancy cars. I would trust Jean-Pierre with my life, but he's also as calculating and political as they come. The real reason for this opportunity—and it's a true opportunity, make no mistake—is Clyde Warden and Dink MacIntosh. Jean-Pierre's been with Dorsen six or seven years now, and he's already fired Clyde twice and Dink three times that I know of.

For what? asked Wynn, all innocence.

For insubordination, said One-Eye. For showing up at a race track so drunk it's a wonder they could fire up their cars. For crashing cars. For doing all the things that Clyde and Dink are famous for doing. Jean-Pierre's always hired them back, though. He's a generous man, but there are two things he can't forgive. One is Clyde and Dink not winning races for Dorsen. The other is Clyde and Dink winning races for someone else—for Ford or Chrysler or General Motors.

One-Eye, he tells me, I fly back to Detroit on Monday morning and my boss has spread a carpet so he can call me in on it, a special Jean-Pierre Andriotti carpet.

Jean-Pierre, he says, have we got the best cars on the Circuit?

Yes, I tell him.

And are Clyde Warden and Dink MacIntosh the two best drivers on the Circuit?

12

Yes, I tell him again.

And at the shop in Ashley Oaks, do the boys there lack for anything?

No, I tell him.

And does Research and Development up here in Motor City stay ahead of the game? Give you speed parts nobody else has? Give you dyno tests and wind-tunnel tests? Even figure out a cheater gas tank? Those back-yard mechanics down there don't know everything, right?

Yes, yes, yes, yes, yes, I say.

So why didn't we win the race? asks my boss.

Because our two hero drivers walled their race cars, I respond.

And why did they do that, Jean-Pierre?

Because they were funnin' each other and didn't watch out where they were going.

So what kind of people are you dealing with down there?

Well, sir, they swung down out of the trees.

One-Eye paused for the laughter. Even Wylie cracked a smile.

Andriotti's tired of dealing with gorillas, said One-Eye to Wynn and me. He's worn out working with legends. Someday down the road he'd like to hire himself a real race-car driver.

. . .

So I am not now racing, not at eight o'clock on a dew-filled Saturday morning. Neither am I scrubbing tires.

My car moves easily to the top lane as I straight-line up the second half of the dogleg toward turn one. I glance at the black box sitting on the floorboard beside me. It is exactly one foot square and four inches high. A dozen wires protrude, seven of them attached to the car and five to me. According to Andriotti, this is a test of a new car on a new race track. The probes measure engine temperature, shock travel, spring loading, weight transfer, sway and anti-sway. All to help build a better, safer, faster Dorsen race car.

And to tell you how the kiddies treat the cars and handle the pressure, I had mumbled while strapping up.

Andriotti didn't respond except to raise his left eyebrow and look mildly hurt. But it's obvious, at least to me, that we're doing more than testing cars and trying out to be a gofer, especially now that Dink is dead and to my knowledge Andriotti's yet to hire up a new chauffeur. This is our audition, Wynn's and mine. A lightning flick of the dice and one of us is headed for the stars, the other back to driving dirt and dreaming others' dreams. Are Wynn and I destined to be tied together forever, just as were our fathers?

There's a tiggle of understeer. To set the car for turns, I have to yank the wheel once more often than I'd like, to break the tires loose and set the car adrifting to the cushion of air travel inches off the concrete walls. Meeting the air is the same as falling into a pile of fresh-cut hay or being wrapped in a woolly blanket. I run down the back chute as close to that wall as I can get—oh, maybe I'll fall off it a little—and there I'm protected and secure, as safe and happy as I ever was in momma's arms.

Three laps left, the signal. Two laps; one. I pass the pits to start my last hot lap and sneak a glance through the creamy dogwoods to the far side of the track. Wynn's car grumbles low on the backstretch, warming up. I quickly overtake him and wave in quick salute, then scream through three and four and kick the apex. One-Eye waves me in, perfunctorily. Andriotti clicks his watches a final time. Reluctantly, I hit the kill switch on the steering column and coast in sudden silence.

When I reach the pits and stop, Bent Nose quickly probes each tire to measure temperature and wear. Red Face writes down the numbers, which I pray will confirm the understeer I've felt, then shows them to One-Eye and Andriotti, not to me.

I sit, not bothering to unstrap, very much alone, and a strange discomfort floods over me. Where is Wylie? He should be here to witness this, for he would find a satisfaction in this trial of his son. So I think. But Wylie cannot be here, of course. Of course. He lies in cold ground, buried with little grief, so says his only progeny, not two weeks from this day.

* * *

Once, when I was eight or nine or ten and scavenging through our house, I found a treasure. It was a black cardboard box about the size of the one on the floorboard next to me now, wrapped with a faded pink ribbon. Inside the box was a photo album, the tiny snapshots mounted with black corners on the heavy, musty pages. One picture I remember above all others. Wylie is holding a baby no more than four months old, and the baby is me. We are in the back yard of our house. In the background is our latticed porch, darkly screened against the heavy summer sun. Wylie wears a light-colored shirt, long-sleeved, open at the neck, its collar stiffly starched. Though I am naked, Wylie holds me close, and my tiny hands reach out for his bobbing Adam's apple. A crescent of a smile breaks my face. Wylie is lean, sturdy, gentle: fatherly. The angle of the picture gives prominence to a slight balding spot at the very top of his head. We are clearly taken with one another. Later—was it days, weeks, years?—I tried again to find the picture box, but it was gone. Such is memory that I now remember not only the details of the photograph but as well the taking of the picture. Wylie held me close, and I grasped for his brilliant eyes, his slender nose, the rough stubble of his chin, and his bobbing throat. Click.

A box of photographs hidden from me forever.

CHAPTER
2

The tricks of memory. Another picture, this one brown and washed in brilliant white, from that once-viewed long-lost treasure trove. Standing in the back are Wylie, my father; Uncle Julian, Wylie's brother, younger by a year; and One-Eye. Sitting on a bench shyly are Wylie's wife, my mother, whom all forever called Miss Ma (more easily pronounced by babes than Helen, and so it came to be); and Aunt Melvina, slick Julian's lovely birdsong. I, a child of four years and five months, and One-Eye's daughter Annalise, a pouty girl of six, kneel in front. On either side of us two children, sitting on the ground, are Heyward Scrivens, flush with newfound wealth and prominence, and Dozier McCartle, Heyward's half brother, the sheriff of the county. Memory is a twist of witness and later explanation, the final coil wrapped once more with fond desire for how we wish the thing to be. How else can I recall with such certitude the cloth of my childhood?

· · ·

Wylie came home from the wars in September of 1945. He was one of the first to go, from Four Corners, and one of the first to get back. He didn't have to go. Being the head of household and the father of a young son, he could have gotten out if he had wanted. But that wasn't Wylie's way. When the time came, he told Miss Ma he wouldn't feel right staying behind when everybody else in the county not blind or lame was going off, and some who were. Miss Ma knew better than to raise a shout. Wylie was fun and foolish, but when he set his mind, there was no way to change it short of mayhem. So off he went, leaving on a bus from the depot next to Miss Dee's small cafe with ten or twelve other boys from the county, all full of themselves, and three and a half years later he came back. On the same damned bus, by the looks of it. Only this time he got off by himself. There had been a lot of telegrams to Four Corners during the time Wylie was away.

He came back a genuine war hero. Two Purple Hearts were his, and a Bronze Star and a citation for a Silver Star, and a passel of campaign ribbons. Once, in the middle of it, there was a picture in the *Stokes County Monitor* that showed him being decorated by a colonel. But the strange thing is, the war Wylie fought took place in a part of the world nobody had heard of before. Most of the men we knew went to Europe. Wylie, though, was in places like Guadalcanal and Tarawa and Majuro and Kume Island and Iwo Jima and Okinawa that we could hardly find on the maps. As the war came near its end, it seemed to us as though the fighting in Europe was getting easier and easier, with the Americans and the British on one side and the Russians on the other squeezing and squeezing until there was nothing left to squeeze. Where Wylie was, however, the war seemed to get worse and worse. We knew it was going to end only when they dropped the bombs and it ended. And Wylie came home.

There were six of us to meet Wylie. One-Eye was there with Annalise, who wore a pink dress so pretty and soft that even I had to admire it.

Don't you touch me with your dirty hands, Andrew Mavis, she said.

It's just a dress, I said. Can't play games in a dress.

Uncle Julian and Aunt Melvina were there. And of course Miss Ma was there, with me.

It was a hot, dry, dusty day, and the old green bus rolled up right in the middle of the hottest part. One-Eye and Uncle Julian had painted a big banner—WELCOME HOME WYLIE MAVIS—and had planned to unfurl it just as Wylie stepped off the bus. But the excitement was too much. No sooner had the bus door wheezed open and One-Eye and Uncle Julian had begun to show the banner than we broke ranks, the six of us, and mad-dashed toward the bus.

Then we stopped. I don't know why. But something made us stop, and so we stopped.

Wylie wasn't wearing his uniform. This was a military bus, and it had started out, we knew, from Terminus with about forty-five soldiers, dropping them off in ones and twos at the small towns north of Terminus up into the mountains. By the time the bus reached Four Corners, it was half full still, but Wylie was the only soldier in his civilian clothes. He might as well have been a farmer. Then there were his eyes. Wylie had the brightest, bluest eyes, like jewels, really, and when he smiled they'd turn even brighter and bluer, if that were possible, their sparkle controlled by some internal rheostat. His eyes were still

19

blue, but now they were a blue the color of cold steel. He looked at the six of us, and as the bus popped and belched and pulled away through the shimmering heat, we could feel the chilling darkness of his stare.

Miss Ma stepped forward.

Wylie, she said. Wylie?

There were tears down her cheeks when she ran to him.

The other adults ventured forth, and that seemed to warm the ice some. Annalise and I hung back, until Miss Ma picked me up and carried me to Wylie.

This here's your son, Wylie, she said, and handed me over.

Wylie took me and held me gently close, like he would a neighbor's child, and looked into my eyes. I don't know whether it was his eyes or the fact of meeting a man who, though I sensed our bondage, was a stranger still, but I began to cry. Not a loud cry, more of a whimper, and I struggled and squirmed to get away.

Wylie set me down. I ran to Uncle Julian, who withered with embarrassment.

Must be the excitement, said Uncle Julian after a silence.

Must be, said Wylie. They's nothing to worry about.

That's what Wylie said, but his pulsing jaw told otherwise.

Let's get on over to your house, One-Eye said to Wylie. Miss Ma and Melvina have the makings of a good dinner waiting. It must be a time since you've had a four-square meal.

Had a pretty good one on the train last night, said Wylie.

We all drove over to our house in Julian's De Soto, a spanking, gleaming machine, though three years old, that smelled of fresh-cured leather.

Wylie seemed more relaxed at dinner, though not by much. Annalise and I played in the living room as we'd done every day since we were old enough not to tear out each other's hair. I cocked an ear for table talk while the adults devoured Aunt Melvina's pot roast and begged Wylie to tell about the places he'd been and the things he'd seen and done.

You get hurt bad, honey? asked Miss Ma.

Not bad, said Wylie.

But they give you them two medals for getting hurt, said Uncle Julian.

Could have given five or six.

What were those islands like? One-Eye asked.

Yes, said Aunt Melvina, were there palm trees and pretty girls?

They wasn't no women and they wasn't no palm trees, said Wylie. And they wasn't really no islands, some of them places. More like rocks sticking up out of the water.

Then why was you fighting for them? asked Julian.

The airfields, said Wylie. The Japs had them and we wanted them back.

That was about the only time Wylie spoke two sentences, except when he took out after Uncle Julian.

You look mighty prosperous, said Wylie to his brother. The war treat you and the women all right, did it?

Now, Wylie, said Aunt Melvina. You know Julian couldn't go. His lungs never have been right.

Let it be, said Uncle Julian softly. Yes, Wylie, I

21

guess you could say I done all right. I wished everything I could be over there with you and the others. I hope you appreciate that.

Mmmm, said Wylie in response.

Julian's got himself a good business deal going with Heyward, One-Eye said.

Heyward Scrivens? asked Wylie. He still run the mill?

He does, One-Eye said. And I'm to tell you your job's waiting just as soon as you want it back.

Wylie looked hard across the table, first to One-Eye and then to Uncle Julian.

You're the first mill hand, he said by way of Julian, who I ever seen with a brand-new-looking De Soto. Must be cutting a lot of trees.

It's more than trees, said Uncle Julian uneasily. We'll talk about it sometime.

Mmmm, said Wylie once again.

Before he could pursue this line of talk, we heard a light knock at the door. Annalise and I ran to it just as Heyward walked through.

I heard you were back, he said to Wylie, and I'm mighty glad to see you. Come by and see me when you can. Julian? We need to talk, right now.

Uncle Julian rose and the two men walked outside. Julian returned alone and gulped down his half-filled cup of coffee.

Got to go, he said. Melvina, I'll leave the car.

Damn, said Wylie when he'd gone. After three and a half years you'd think my only brother would stay at least through dessert. Him and Heyward both.

It's a little business deal, said One-Eye. They've a little business to attend.

Soon the others took their leave, figuring, so I later came to understand, that Wylie and Miss Ma had some catching up to do. I was shushed and sent to my room, though fall of night was far away. There I listened through thin walls to mounting sounds of passion give way to sad frustration. They had been apart too long and fumbled once again as youngblood virgins. Shyness was not the cause of their discontent, but absence—absence and the timeless wish for things to be as once before they had been, even as they knew they could not quickly close the gap of a thousand missing nights. Sometimes—this, too, I later came to know—desire can be so fierce as to garble up the getting, even in the bedroom. Maybe especially in the bedroom.

Finally, they stopped trying. Uncomprehending, I heard Miss Ma try to soothe Wylie's fragile ego with patient words of sympathy, then fall into a calming sleep. Wylie spent the night in shallow rest. With each nocturnal sound, a cricket, or a distant barking dog, he woke full awake to sweat and shiver both at once. Near dawn he left their common bed and, pulling on a pair of trousers, walked softly to the kitchen. He turned on the single light. Its dim glow cast dark shadows on the pale yellow walls. He opened a cabinet, found a bottle, and on his pants he slowly wiped away the years of ancient dust. He got a glass and poured himself three fingers, neat, of soothing bitter nectar and swallowed them down. Then he sat in a kitchen chair and poured himself another. He arranged the bottle and the glass before him, but declined a further touch of either. Miss Ma, watching unseen from the dark shadows, saw in Wylie's eyes a hollow stare she'd never seen before. He was there, yet he wasn't there. It was as though he had found some deep dark corner of his memory, one very far away, and yet so real that it had captured a part of Wylie's soul forever.

Miss Ma wanted to run to Wylie and hug him hard, so that he would come back to her, all of him, and they would be just as they had been once so long before. But as silently as she had come she returned to their bed, there to smother the sobs she knew that Wylie never would have heard.

I, too, slept in shallow sleep that night and bore my distant witness. Though then I could not know of all that I had heard and seen, I wondered at the sudden stranger in our midst, one once so dear to me and now so far away.

CHAPTER
3

What Wylie came back to, late that summer of 1945, was not much different from what he had left. Four Corners had an unincorporated population of 493, about one-fifth of the county of which it was the seat. Its name came from State Highway 77, two lanes of blacktop that twisted down from the Quahills, low and worn and shrouded in perpetual blue-gray haze, and then straightened out in the plain for the run to Terminus; and from Stokes Boulevard, though nobody could remember it ever being a true boulevard, which crossed east to west, from nowhere to nowhere. Four Corners was a child of geography. In the foothills, isolated, the town had little to draw people in and less to keep them there.

Well, then, so there we were.

The cobbled intersection was actually a traffic circle, for in its center was a ten-foot bronze statue, on a three-foot cement base, of Colonel Winslow Allgood Stokes, who stood with his right leg up on a rock and stared to the distant mountains. A plaque informed one and all that Col. Stokes (1832–1901) had been commissioned a captain in the Army of Tennessee in the summer of 1863, breveted to colonel at Resaca, captured and paroled at New Hope Church in late May of the following year.

One-Eye said his daddy remembered the Colonel, who, after giving the county its name, lived out his life in splendid isolation in a small whitewashed house at the eastern end of Stokes Boulevard. Every Confederate Memorial Day while the Colonel, by then a kind, befuddled soul, was alive, a wreath mysteriously appeared at the base of the statuary and the Colonel would parade for one hour, no more, his brass buttons gleaming, his sparkling bayonet at the ready.

My daddy was a suspicious cuss, said One-Eye, and once on the eve of Memorial Day he staked out the old Colonel's house. Sure enough, past darkness when the Colonel was sure none could see, he brought the wreath himself and laid it ceremoniously at the base of his own monument.

On the northwest corner of the square was Billy Winslow's General Store. A potbellied wood stove, which potbellied Billy kept fired winter and summer, sat squat in the center, and you could buy everything from bubble gum to feed grain. Billy's was also the telegraph office and Billy was the county postmaster. A Winslow had been postmaster for as long as anyone could remember. Potbellied Billy never seemed to age or change, true of many there. Four Corners folks were hurried to maturity, then wore out, grew tired, ceased to grow.

On the southwest corner was the Stokes County courthouse, where Sheriff Dozier McCartle held forth. The courthouse was low and brown-bricked and had but three rooms. Dozier occupied one. In the second, the county clerk kept track of passages. The third was a three-cell jail. Caleb Jones was Dozier's one and only deputy, his job obtained in large measure because he was Dozier's nephew—that, and difficulty in imagining Caleb at other work. Caleb, in fact, was rarely observed working at all. He had neither office nor room. If he was in the courthouse free of duties, which was most of the time, he usually could be found in one of the cells, sleeping. The jail was rarely occupied. Occasionally, Dozier or Caleb would pick up a drunk and let him sleep it off in the safety of a cell. If there was cause to hold a real criminal, just as likely he would be sent to Terminus until a circuit judge appeared and the apparatus of a trial could be assembled.

Crossing over the street to the southeast was the *Stokes County Monitor*. The weekly paper's publisher, editor, and advertising director was Henry Stokes, no relation to the Colonel so far as Henry knew. Henry wrote the stories and badgered for the ads, and two days weekly One-Eye set the type. Glorious days, those were, for Annalise and me. We got there early to watch One-Eye heat the hot-lead Linotype, then observed transfixed as he lightly fingered the keys and pulled the levers of the tinkling, massive machine.

Make me my name, said Annalise.

Me, too, said I.

With feigned reluctance always, One-Eye would. His hands danced the keyboard, tripped the lever, and soon the soft-lead slug shot down into the tray, our names backward and mirror-imaged:

ANNALISE MARIE RIVERS

ANDREW BENTON MAVIS

The slugs were as heavy as gold, more precious. I must have a hundred of them, precious still.

Setting type's a way to learn an education, One-Eye would say, if you don't go buggy cross-eyed first.

Dorothy's Cafe completed the square at the northeast corner, though it was known to all simply as Miss Dee's. Dorothy Robinson's cafe gave lunch six days a week, from eleven till two, closed Sundays, ordinary fare. Five nights the week, however, Tuesday through Saturday, it was quite a different place and served but one meal: steak and tamales and salad. Nothing more.

Miss Dee's used to be a regular dinner restaurant, but one night in the war a stranger happened by as Miss Dee fixed to pull the shades and stack the chairs.

We're closed, she said. I'm out of food.

I've driven for six hours and haven't eaten in ten, said the stranger, polite but firm.

Miss Dee pondered and a twinkle flamed her eye. She had a T-bone steak in stock, and in her freezer these six tamales taking space. She guessed at how to fix them, since tamales weren't a basic staple in our parts. She brought the plate—one steak and six tamales—and watched the stranger wolf them down in silence.

Miss Dee, he said with uncorraled delight, I have just finished the best meal of my life, positively.

Miss Dee, no fool, the next day hied to Terminus and returned, her car slung low with—need I say? It took scant weeks for word to spread, and in the month Miss Dee's was famous for a hundred miles around. No reservations taken, you couldn't get in the place unless you showed at six, her evening hours being then till ten.

Miss Dee never hired help, except a boy or girl from the town to clean the tables, wash the dishes. She took and cooked all orders by herself. Miss Dee's wasn't big. Once a year Heyward would get on her to expand, and once a year Miss Dee said no. The fifteen tables, each with ketchup, A-1 sauce, and salt and pepper shakers, were just right, not too big and not too small.

There was more to Four Corners: Heyward Scrivens's mill, the county consolidated school, the volunteer fire department, and such. But if you hung around the Corners four you'd get a quick idea of what was going on.

The social center was Miss Dee's. Even between two and six when it was closed, it never was. There would be somebody at the tables sipping coffee or sugar tea, or chewing fat and passing by the hours. Dozier went there when the law-and-order front was quiet, and Heyward.

Heyward was a solid man, without an ounce of fat, or hair. Eighty percent, I'd say, was natural attrition; the rest he shaved daily, pointing out the barber savings. He wore sunglasses day and night, indoors and out, in brilliant light of midday sun and gloomy dark of storm. He wore a leather vest in all the seasons, and a baseball cap. Though he owned the mill and ran as well another business, what he mostly did was sit at one of Miss Dee's tables, sipping coffee in the winter months and sugar tea in summer, nothing else. Indeed, by Heyward's choice of beverage was the yearly change of seasons twice foretold. There comes a day in early spring when a softness to the air tells winter's done, and in the fall, the opposite. Heyward knew those days.

Miss Dee, he'd say, I think I'll have my sugar tea today.

Or:

Miss Dee, put on the water for my coffee.

29

On cue, the seasons changed. Heyward could read the winds.

Heyward and Dozier were half brothers. Between them they held Four Corners in a crusty barnacle's grip.

Heyward Scrivens was the firstborn in this century, in the county, and the first to lose his daddy. He arrived at 3:17 on the morning of January 1, 1900, in the bedroom of the Scrivenses' dirt-farm country cabin. To honor this occasion, Heyward Sr. found a decent whiskey bottle, and more than less he simply wandered off. Polly Scrivens knew her husband much too well to query such an absence, and his generally frozen body was found a short day later in a neighbor's woodshed.

Polly's luck with men was not profound. Undismayed by Heyward Sr.'s sudden absence, she soon was joined with Charles McCartle. From this union Dozier sprang, in 1902, gangle-limbed at birth, as now, but he no more than Heyward claims a memory of his father. Polly explained to both her boys, later on, that in her opinion the world was just too much for Charles, and one day he simply left with word that he was off to Terminus. Polly thought she saw him there once, but could not be sure and had no tugging desire to pursue the matter further.

The boys were close, growing up, though Heyward always led.

I come into this world two years ahead of him, Heyward would say in rare moments of introspection, and no matter how old we got it seemed as though he always stayed those two years in arears.

Polly moved to Four Corners, the boys in tow. With some family money and what she got from the sale of the farm—she acquired Heyward Sr.'s by common law, and Charles never laid claim to the place he lived so shortly in

—she opened a boardinghouse and raised her sons as best she could. She was a looker, Polly—no movie queen, but fine enough—and she had what then in quaintness was called a roving eye. Heyward Sr. and Charles had disinclined her for a third trip to the altar, but the boys recalled the nights when a boarder wouldn't stay forever in the bed in which he'd first retired. Displeased though they were, Heyward and Dozier came to understand and tolerate, though it's hard to say coincidence alone caused neither one to marry in his time. Dozier played around, we knew; if Heyward fell, the secret's stayed with him, save for rumors of a youthful passion for Miss Dee. Whatever . . . Polly, Heyward, and Dozier set themselves apart. They worked a different value stick that few in town tried earnestly to understand.

Polly prepared the boys for her leave-taking, which occurred the exact date of Dozier's eighteenth birthday: February 22, 1920. She loved celebrations, none more than birthdays, hers and theirs, and on that fated date she said she'd met a man from Terminus. And now, she said, that both her sons had realized maturity and proved themselves capable of living lives on their own, she would try to make up, to herself, the missing years. Goodbye. Heyward and Dozier would always be welcome in her new home. But, goodbye.

It might have been the saddest birthday in their lives, but no. Tears fell, for sure, but Polly had done her work well. There are many kinds of love, I'm told: one to draw two souls together; another to prepare for separation and release. The latter kind was Polly's love, and came the dawn of her departure, the boys were there to wish her well, all cheers.

Soon after, Heyward sat his younger brother down and

drew the map that told how they would come to rule the town.

There's two kinds of power in this and any other hamlet big or small, said Heyward, economic power and political power. I'll take the first and you the second, and there we'll have it.

Just like that? asked doubtsome Dozier.

Just like that, said stolid Heyward. In our time.

Okay, bro', said Dozier. Show me the how of it.

Heyward did. The immediate problem, of course, was that at the time of their divvy-up chatterings, Heyward was not yet twenty-one and Dozier only inches beyond eighteen. Heyward, though he knew the value of a dollar—I don't ever remember him without a roll, though ofttimes of the smallish sort—had few to name, just then, while Dozier was not exactly a political potent.

But Heyward laid it out, as he and Brother Dozier never tired of telling, and in due time the thing did come to pass as he had planned.

Since Polly's new man was prosperous enough, she turned her savings, a $3,000 amount, all to Heyward. Who looked around at what the county had to offer and turned to timber, a business best not touched unless the gambler lurks within. With Dozier's slack-jawed acquiescence, Heyward took the $3,000, every final penny, and bought a tract of timber up in the northern end of the county that nobody knew about. He cut the timber and he held it from the market till the price was doubly right; in six months' time the three G's had become six, which, in 1920, went a fine long distance. For ten years Heyward brokered thusly, though his line of success was sometimes incomplete. Once, while holding timber, he read the market wrong and had to deliver at half the price he'd paid. Busted flat, he was, but by that time the banks in Terminus knew him well, a speculator true and honest, and soon the greenback flow resumed.

Lord, said Dozier by way of rehash, I remember one venture. There was this mountain that some farmer yearned to sell to stop foreclosure, and Heyward got it cheap.

Dozier, he said, up that mountain we're going to build a road and take the timber out.

I thought Heyward crazy, Dozier reminisced. If you've ever cut a mountain road, you'll know it's about the most difficult work there is. Three hours with a crosscut saw and you'll build muscles on your hair, no lie. Well, we cut the road, and on completion I staggered home and slept a night and day. When I awoke, Heyward was gone. I didn't know where. He came back the next day from wherever he had been and announced he'd sold the mountain, now "developed," for three times what he'd paid.

Heyward was smart with numbers and brave with money, but after ten years on the timber roller coaster, he took his considerable profit, his and Dozier's, and started up a pulp mill. His Midas touch remained. In time, the mill became the largest employer in the county. It sat outside the town on Highway 77, north, smelling up the Corners something grim when the wind was wrong.

Dozier's role took longer to fulfill. In the absence of a city charter, the sheriff held all power over daily life and death within his jurisdiction, and that's what Heyward had in mind for Brother D.

Now, don't you get impatient on me, Heyward said. Your time will come.

When Dozier wasn't cutting timber or helping Heyward in other ways, he got deputized. Then followed a "donation" to the county treasury by Heyward, and Dozier was appointed the deputy sheriff full time. The sheriff then was Carl Givens, a kindly soul who mainly sat on a shade-tree bench beneath the statuary and told stories on the memory of the Colonel. If he issued six warrants a year, he rambled loud and long of overwork. In 1932, when Dozier was an even thirty, Carl suddenly resigned to work for Heyward at the mill for twice a sheriff's meager pay, and Dozier, unopposed, was nominated and elected to the vacancy.

Perfect timing, all of this, as Heyward knew.

By 1932 the bottom had fallen out of the timber business and nearly every other save but one—the drinking business. If anything, the hard times gave a kick to that particular sector of the economy. Now, the making of mountain whiskey was not unknown to Stokes County in the time so named, much to the dismay of Will Rollins, the preacher at the Baptist church in town, as well as certain of his faithful, but mostly it was farmers who would run a batch for home consumption and casual sale to their neighbors. Heyward saw another way, and in so doing got him and Dozier through the hard years fine, and if the truth be known, the rest of the county as well.

It was a simple deal, really. Heyward, with the business sense, would supply the whiskey, act as middleman between the source and market. Not Four Corners, no. Heyward had eyes for bigger game than that.

I started small and careful, Heyward said, and for the longest time I never got much bigger. I could have, but I had my standards, and while the temptation was great to let them slide, I kept them firm. I had my name to protect, mine and Dozier's.

Heyward's taste test was county-famous. When Heyward got the word that one of his suppliers had run a batch and bottled it, he'd go—not to the still, but to the stash. Heyward had a head for numbers, as I've said, but his sense of direction wasn't worth a badger's fart. Dozier, on the far hand, knew where every county still was and had been. Part of this was more than understood, despite the secret nature of the trade. On some days there'd be seen a dozen curling wisps of smoke all through the northern mountains, but unless the operators of the stills gave guidance, never likely, the secrets held. Take Waylon Kelley, an ancient mountain man who supplied Heyward true and regular. All knew where Waylon lived and the definitions of his property, and all knew where meandered the coil-cooling stream near which his still would have to be. Yet, none save Dozier ever found it.

And it wasn't but fifty yards from the old man's cabin, Dozier liked to say by way of interjection. He hid it so well.

So Heyward, say, would go to Waylon's stash, and there before him might be stacked a hundred gallons of silk-smooth liquid corn. With sudden arbitration, Heyward pointed. Waylon fetched the designated jug and poured three fingers into each of two glasses, a ceremony fraught with trust and fiscal import. Then Heyward invited Waylon to drink one down. When Waylon finished, Heyward did the same, and waited. And if nothing happened more than pleasant buzzes—imagine butterflies escaping from your skull—the deal then was struck.

The taste test took its toll, though, which perhaps explains why never have I seen but sugar tea and coffee cross Heyward's lips in public.

Dozier's job was twofold. One was to keep the

county free of outside influence, meaning, of course, the law—except, again of course, for Dozier's presence. The other was to see that Heyward worked with those within the county as he chose. Heyward wasn't the only entrepreneur in those parts. He wasn't greedy. What he wanted was Stokes County. What went on in neighboring counties was none of his business. Dozier made sure that the other whiskey linchpins didn't make Stokes County any business of their own. Then, too, there was always the risk of freelancers from within the county, but these never stayed in business long. Dozier and Caleb simply shut them down, usually at drawing-off time, when the hurt was worst. He and Caleb would go to the freelance still with sledgehammers and axes and then there wouldn't be a still there anymore.

These raids, though few, served a double purpose. They gave strong notice to Heyward's suppliers, and they allowed Dozier to show the state and federal revenuers—whoever happened to show the interest—that he had firm handle on his county's whiskey trade. Most everybody understood, though, that the deals Heyward made were fair and true, and trouble from within was minimal.

For this protection, Dozier earned full ten percent of Heyward's profit after overhead, a princely supplement for the two-years younger brother.

This, then, is what Wylie came back to.

Supply, for Heyward, was little problem, by the main, once Waylon Kelley and the others saw that an acre of corn whiskey drew treble on the market than did an acre of corn. The market, though, at which gazed Heyward's eyes, was Terminus. Business picked up in the war, no surprise. Terminus was a major railroad center, and all the maps showed no bigger city for two hundred miles in every direction. After the war, business got even better. All the men and boys came back—those who did come back—with back-pay jangle money in their pockets, looking hard for easy ways to spend it. Terminus was dry, as, indeed, was the state, but that was no prevention to the purchase of elixir by those who drank in downtown neon clubs and lily mansions both. Terminus, though, was seventy-two alien miles away; and here's where One-Eye clambered in.

One-Eye never drove a whiskey car, not even before the accident that gave him his fond name, but there has never been a man who's known his way around machines, including and particularly cars, better than he. To a stranger, One-Eye danced the Linotype two days a week and in the rest of time kept Heyward's mill machinery tuned. At the first, that's all One-Eye did. The fellows who whiskey-tripped for Heyward drove their own cars. But as the years went on, and as the various aspects of the law looked into what was going on in Stokes County, and elsewhere, it became a necessity to modify the cars somewhat.

A typical load of whiskey was a hundred gallons, to keep the numbers even, each one in a Mason jar and weighing nearly seven pounds. These next seven hundred pounds put a fierce, complaining strain on the cars, mainly Fords from the pre-war years. The straining cars, in turn, put a strain on the trippers, once the revenuers and the sheriffs—excepting Dozier—came out after them. The pay for a run to Terminus and back was a flat fifty dollars, good extra money, and maybe some drivers could cadge two trips a week, more in season. But the money couldn't start to compensate should a sheriff shoot a radiator or some such. So by evolution, call it, and in particular right after the war, it was a necessary thing to prepare a car for a trip run. One-Eye let his work slide at the mill and went full-time into the business, for Heyward.

He'd go to Terminus and buy a '32 or '34 or '36 junker —the '39 Ford Standard was best, for some reason—for a hundred dollars and less, and tow it back to the mill, where Heyward had created a couple of rooms. In two weeks, working by himself, One-Eye would have the junker in such fine shape that Henry Ford himself couldn't have recognized the product. One-Eye took out everything on the inside but the driver's seat. He put heavy-duty springs over the rear axle to accommodate the extra weight. He might even borrow the rear-end gear assembly from a pickup truck and transplant it to that little light sedan, then fix it up with heavy-duty tires. He covered the radiator with boiler plate and oversized the gas tank, to make sure a tripper wouldn't have to stop in the middle of a run. Finally, One-Eye would go to the engine and plain tinker. And tinker. And tinker some more. When he was through and kicked over the ignition, that car, with its rear end sitting high like an iron mare ready to receive her silver stallion, would tremble, and you'd swear that nice old Ford, or whatever it was, would want to fly. Which, of course, was the basic idea.

Some cars he'd make different. These were the set-off cars, which the people in Terminus who bought Heyward's product used to deliver the whiskey to the local retailers one or two, maybe three gallons at a place. The trip cars were for the long haul; the set-off cars were jack-rabbits designed for quick acceleration in close quarters. But One-Eye didn't make those cars for Heyward. That was the end phase of the operation and Heyward didn't concern himself with it much.

My job is to get the whiskey to Terminus, Heyward liked to say. What happens to it after that is someone else's worry.

CHAPTER

Wylie Mavis took up tripping because Jason Martin was an idiot.

There were all varieties of transporters: young men and old; straight-arrow family men; and Saturday-night bachelors; men caught up in the thrills and chills and others lured by the money. There were full-time trippers who made three and four runs a week into Terminus and part-timers who filled in when a regular was out of sorts or in jail or had lost his car, and who might make but one run a month or so, just to keep their senses keen. They had their different styles, and at Miss Dee's or on the iron bench beneath the far-off gaze of bronzed Colonel Stokes there'd be some fine arguments about the best way to get in the load. That was the important thing, getting in the load, because if you didn't, you weren't paid. Worse than not getting in the load was losing the car, which was more or less a cardinal sin and hard to live down. If a car fell down, or crashed, or got run so tight it had to be abandoned, it came out of the tripper's own pocket, meaning a severe shortfall of around three months, give or take. For this reason, the trippers were never too far ahead of the game, though some stayed farther ahead than others.

Basically, though, when all the talk was over, there were two kinds of trippers. One type was quiet, sneaky; then there were the crazies.

Uncle Julian, the transporter, was of the former persuasion, like Uncle Julian, the man. One-Eye prepared the cars to taste, and you couldn't have told Uncle Julian's was a whiskey car if you'd seen it sitting in a dealer's showroom. It was a Cadillac, and while One-Eye had ripped out the back seat—the whiskey had to be stored someplace—it did have a front seat. When Uncle Julian tripped, he dressed up in a funeral suit and a fedora, and sometimes, for appearance's sake, he'd bring along a passenger, usually Aunt Melvina. Who could figure that a man and his wife spiffed up like they were headed off to church were carrying a load, even if it was three o'clock in the a.m.? Julian did ask One-Eye to tune that Caddy to within an inch of its steel-bodied life, just in case, but it had a muffler and ran so quietly that he could motor past a police station without raising suspicion. Which he did many times, making sure.

He ran at dusk and stayed fifty-fifty to the back roads, which he knew as well as the streets of Four Corners. In all his years of running, he never lost a load, never lost a car, never even got a speeding ticket. That didn't contrive to make him a legend in his own time, like some, but it did wonders for his bankroll. Quiet, sneaky, he ran; quiet, sneaky, he was.

Jason Martin's car was a trip car, you could tell. It was one of those 1939 Ford Standards hotted up six ways to Sunday with big fat tires, heavy-duty springs, an oversized engine, a cut-out exhaust to bypass the muffler on the open road. That baby quivered and shivered at rest. Jason called it *Thunder*, even had the name painted on the dashboard, and it was a trip car, no mistake. I'd lie in bed and hear the roar and know that Jason was setting out. Or coming back in.

Jason lived by himself in a house no more than a shack on the outskirts of town, beyond the mill, and to hear Julian tell, which he often did, Jason didn't have the sense God awarded goslings. He drank moonshine for a start, and there were few in the whiskey business who'd touch the stuff, particularly in the years right after the war when business stiffened up and the moonshiners didn't pay the attention to quality control that they might have.

He tried to enlist in the Marines when Wylie signed himself, passing for eighteen though four years shy of that. He would have made it, too, except his momma and his poppa caught the bus in Terminus as it closed its doors for Parris Island, and passed the recruiter his birth certificate. Next day, he took up diggings by himself, and Heyward, sensing promise, soon had him tripping regularly.

Jason purposely tried to get run. You could tell the measure of his trip by looking at him at Miss Dee's. If he returned hunched over and sad, you knew that nothing much had happened. But if he strolled in bright and perky, you'd be sure that he had found some trouble on the way. The best news he could say was that he'd led a merry chase the entire seventy-two miles, both directions.

He chose to run in daylight, leaving nighttime passages to others. If nobody picked up on him by the time he'd blown to Madison, halfway in, he'd stop for coffee in the center of that town and more or less announce that he was loaded down. Having tossed the gauntlet, he'd be off, and if the lead time he'd arranged was insufficient goad, he'd pull off beside the road and wait for his pursuers to catch him up.

The straightest line to Terminus was Highway 77, but that was rarely Jason's way.

One time he said to those assembled at Miss Dee's, I must have stopped twenty times waiting for those fool sheriffs to find me out. Damn near ran out of gas and patience both.

Quite something. All of One-Eye's cars, with their oversized gas tanks, had a range of two hundred miles, give or take, and for Jason nearly to have run his tank to dryness meant that he had run circles around every town between Four Corners and Terminus, literally.

Jason ran out of luck, or brains, in the spring of '46. He set out at eight one morning, but nobody felt concern when he hadn't returned by night. The figuring was that he had waited somewhere for a good pursuit, or maybe had run across a sporting lady friend in Terminus, not unheard-of.

Jason cashed in, said Dozier, ambling in Miss Dee's the following morn. He wrapped *Thunder* around a tree, north of Madison.

Which way was he heading? Heyward asked, shoving his glasses high atop his glistening dome.

Back home, said Dozier.

He was empty?

Yes, brother, he was.

Who ran him? Heyward asked.

That goddamn sheriff there in Madison who's been after him for years.

But he was empty, said Heyward. Coming home.

You know that was Jason's way, said Dozier. He didn't need to have a load on board to look for sport.

Heyward shrugged. Soon thereafter he approached Uncle Julian about Wylie.

Wylie, who'd been working at the mill since his return, took scant minutes to agree. On April 20, 1946, a date Uncle Julian never forgot, Wylie Mavis ran his first load.

They could have fixed their loads at the mill after the moonshiner had brought in his supply, the way soft-handed Julian preferred. Some 'shiners, however, insisted that the trippers load directly at the stash, Waylon Kelley being one. Early that afternoon, a Saturday, Wylie and Uncle Julian left for Waylon's stash, Julian in his '34 Cadillac and Wylie in the car of his choice, a grumbling Ford.

Wylie named it then and there, said Uncle Julian. It, too, would be a *Thunder—Thunder Too.*

Waylon met them at his cabin, all suspicion.

Greetings, Julian, he said. Who's this?

This here's Wylie, Uncle Julian said. You heard about Jason. Wylie's to replace him.

Those were nearly all the spoken words that afternoon, a long one.

They walked a quarter mile to the stream that slid through Waylon's property and up the stream a hundred yards more to a shed.

Where's the still? asked Wylie.

Don't be looking, Uncle Julian said. You may be standing hard by it. I've been coming here for years. Haven't seen one yet.

Two hundred gallons were inside, bottled. For the

44

next three hours they loaded up. Waylon sat the whole time, watching, declining to help. They moved the jars from stash to cars in mesh sacks, the kind you buy oranges in, eight gallons to the sack, two sacks suspended from an oxbow piece of wood across their shoulders. They laid the jars in a certain way so they wouldn't roll around and break, an art. Wylie was a strong man, stronger by far than Uncle Julian, but after two trips, Uncle thought that Wylie would bail out and call his trip career goodbye right there.

Goddamn, said Wylie, muttering. God-*damn*.

Uncle Julian smiled, having done this work before, but made sure the smile was not for Wylie's eyes to see.

At nightfall, finished, they drove the cars to the mill and went to Miss Dee's for dinner and a lot of coffee. Heyward was there; Dozier wasn't. Whenever one of Heyward's trippers set out, Dozier usually made sure he was an elsewhere place.

Miss Dee remarked to Wylie that it had been a while since he'd been seen in her place.

Wylie, hoarding words, nodded and pointed to his cup. And rubbed his red-raw shoulders.

At ten o'clock they set out, Uncle Julian in his sneaky Cadillac and Wylie in his *Thunder Too*. Julian decided to stay the main road, a sometimes risk. At that time of night you could be nearly certain that any car you saw or heard was a trip car, or the police, particularly if the car was a '34 Ford that sat so low to the ground, loaded down, that a brick could not have space beneath it, super springs and all. On the other hand, while Uncle Julian knew the back roads, Wylie didn't.

Sneaky Julian ran nothing fancy. Leading in his Cadillac with *Thunder Too* a hundred yards behind, he kept the speed needle touching fifty. He watched antsy Wylie in his rearview mirror. A couple of times Wylie ran up on Uncle Julian's bumper and motioned Uncle to speed up. Uncle motioned Wylie right back into place. The single time they left the highway was near Madison, because of the sheriff there. Uncle Julian sort of went this way and that way and swung around the town on country roads with trees and bushes hanging close enough to touch. Eerie, but safe; Uncle Julian's way.

They got to Terminus in ninety minutes' time and drove to their drop-off, a house on the northern outskirts. They drove up a twisting, gravel driveway and into an open garage, whose door silently closed behind them. Inside, two men from the shadows scraped dirt and slid back a false wooden floor just enough to allow the unloading of the cars. Then they slid the floor back, replaced the dirt, and made financial remuneration: five hundred dollars total, of which Wylie and Uncle Julian would each keep fifty. The rest was Heyward's to split with Waylon Kelley, and with Dozier.

Finished.

That all there is to it? questioned Wylie.

Yes, so far, said Uncle Julian. You'd best hope that's all there ever is to it.

If disappointed, Wylie covered well, until . . .

Not more than three or four miles out of Terminus, headed back, Wylie suddenly roared up beside Uncle Julian and stayed even only long enough for his brother to cadge a glancing look.

What I saw was spooky, Uncle Julian later said. Wylie's eyes were silver nuggets, piercing their own light through the evil darkness.

Wylie then was gone, with a quick-start roar that could

have been heard by Allgood Stokes. He didn't smile, didn't wave, just went, and in thirty seconds' time was out of sight. Loaded down, that car of his could move; free of burden, it was an airplane minus wings.

I knew right then, said Uncle Julian, that I had made my last run with Wylie. Oh, we might still set out together, but we would never run together. Wylie was a crazy. He was going to make one fine whiskey tripper or wind up like the driver he'd replaced. Either way, Heyward Scrivens had lost himself a mill hand.

Uncle Julian, sly and quiet, never lost a car, never lost a load, and never got run—but once.

. . .

It caused such a stir that by the time the story made the rounds, which it quickly did, folks would gaily snap a gallus at the simple recollection of it. Slow, sly Julian, his Caddy's needle stuck at fifty, never more, getting run by the *po*-lice. Damn. Of this I need no faded yellow pictures to nudge my memory, for on the day of days that led directly to that night of nights, Uncle Julian chose to bring along as decoy his one and only nephew—me.

I was twelve by then and needed no persuasion, being on the cusp of manhood, or so I thought. Wylie, out of town on new pursuits and through with tripping, was unavailable for consultation, much to Uncle's lingering regret. Miss Ma alone gave her consent.

Uncle Julian picked me up an hour shy of sunset, dapper-dressed in three-piece gray and wearing his fedora at a jaunty angle. His slick-backed hair and pencil mustache glistened with country-club respectability. I, in keeping with his style, wore slacks and jacket and a tightly knotted tie.

The time of year was crisp October. First frost had

brought rich autumn color to the mountains, and we set out just as lowering sun sent brilliant shafts of light through the thicket woods, a light so rich and mellow as to bring surprising sadness to my throat.

My stomach flopped at the thought of our vaguely illicit mission. If Uncle Julian was similarly inclined, he gave no sign. In Madison we saw a sheriff's deputy. Julian waved. On the square he parked his car, careful to leave the motor running, and while beads of sweat trickled down my shirt, he went inside the Rexall there and brought back two ice-cream cones, chocolate for me, strawberry for himself.

I was impressed.

If you feel guilty, Uncle Julian said, you probably are. I don't feel guilty.

From there on in, the trip was joyous and uneventful, though the day had brought out every leaf watcher from Terminus and in a pinch the traffic could have proved a burden. But nobody ran Uncle Julian; nobody ever did. And soon we were in Terminus, the north-side outskirts, where Julian took a side street and gunned his Cadillac up the driveway to the drop. Two men quickly raised the garage door and motioned us inside. The hidden cellar of which I'd heard was then uncovered, and while Uncle Julian and I watched in silence, the pair unloaded the car with quick efficiency.

When they were done, they looked to my direction. No word had yet been spoken.

He's okay, said Uncle Julian. He's Wylie's son.

Grins split the faces of the two. They walked over and shook my hand.

You tell your daddy hello from Jake and Ellie, said

one. Damn, when he was running you could hear *Thunder Too* halfway before he got here.

And then a consultation.

What's up, Ellie? asked Uncle Julian. I've got the kid, should soon be heading back.

We need a set-off driver for the night, said the one called Jake. Leadbelly's been detained by a princess of the night.

Leadbelly, it was explained, was Amos Ledbetter, whose weakness for nocturnal pleasures sometimes conflicted with his work.

Setting off, I soon found out, required different skills from tripping on the open road, and a different car as well. Julian was no stranger to this task, but his nerves weren't really suited.

There'll be an extra hundred for you, said Ellie.

Uncle Julian pondered briefly, checked his watch, succumbed.

He thought of leaving me behind, but figured finally that my presence would be more help than hindrance.

So now another car was loaded up, with pints and half-pints, sometimes quarts and gallons, for delivery to the regular customers on the route, a wedge-shaped sector of the city.

We started out again, though unlike the quiet trip down, Uncle Julian's body was on a full alert, nervous, twitching, glancing at any untoward sight or sound. A Terminus squad car picked us up with half our load delivered. Uncle Julian ceased his setting off and drove around the bright big-city streets with aimless innocence until the car fell off our track, then once again resumed.

On smaller stops, I'd take the whiskey in myself. At

one such place, the Dixie Cafe—I can't forget—I was barely inside when the uneventful night was pierced with wailing sirens and red revolving lights, from two directions.

Let's go, boy, shouted Uncle Julian from the car.

I ran outside and clambered in.

Hang on, Andrew, said Uncle Julian.

Yessir, said I, scared to death and loving every minute.

Cool Julian knew the city better than the cops. That much was soon in evidence. He drove this way and that, jackrabbit lefts and rights that would have done absent Wylie proud. In no time short, we lost our bright and loud pursuers and settled in the weekend revelry of Terminus University, whose campus was convenient to our escape.

Twitching and bemused, we watched the college play for half an hour. Secure again, I'll be damned if Uncle Julian didn't finish up his rounds before he gunned his little car a hundred miles an hour back to the drop.

Any problem? asked Ellie. I heard sirens.

No problem, said Uncle Julian.

Back in Uncle Julian's Cadillac, we veterans of the whiskey trade declined to head directly back, but stopped into a posh and fancy restaurant for some dinner.

Anything you want, said Uncle Julian. It's been a day.

Uncle Julian drew a pocket flask, a side to him I hadn't seen, and popped a swallow, then three more. Through dinner he stayed in silence.

I don't think it would be smart for us to mention what happened tonight, he said when we were through.

Okay, I said. Why not?

Your father might not understand.

He paid the bill, leaving the tip in coins arranged in

a circle on the white tablecloth. The waitress, whom I thought quite beautiful, smiled at us. We took our leave.

The Caddy ran quiet. The road home was silent, though once, with the window cracked enough to rid it of the wind whistle, I thought I heard the distant roar of a trip car. The sound was soothing. Cautious Julian never raised the needle over fifty. The steady dark of night and wheen of whispering tires soon did me in. Slumped against the door, I fell asleep, and dreamed of faraway places and glorious waitresses and Amos Ledbetter with his princess of the night.

. . .

I couldn't keep the secret, not for long. The next day following, I told Wynn the story of my trip with Uncle Julian, swearing him to blood silence. Feeling adult and brave, I embellished where I could, leaving nothing to imagination, of which Wynn, by then my three years' solid friend, had precious little anyway. Though he was impressed by our adventure setting off, the trip itself stirred little in the way of envy or regret, much to my disappointment.

Fifty miles an hour all the way? asked Wynn with scorn. Ice-cream cones on a whiskey run? You wore a tie and fell asleep?

We got the load in, him and me, I said, striving to maintain the upper hand. That's all that counts, no matter how you do it.

But Wynn declined to buy the glory of the deed, made fun, instead.

CHAPTER
5

I punch apart my safety harness, no help from anyone. One-Eye and Jean-Pierre engage in mute, phlegmatic conversation; Bent Nose and Red Face consult their numbers, decline to look my way. I climb sweating from my car. Through the heaving dogwoods, bent low from brisky breeze, suddenly I hear, not see, Wynn's car burp and grumble warming up, impatient to begin. The day is crisp but warming, and will be hot by the apex of the sun. The track will change, I realize, as the oily asphalt bleeds and softens, something to remember. The next time down the back straight, Wynn punches the accelerator, and with a building roar that shatters the pristine morn, he starts his run. The sound rattles off the empty grandstand seats even before Wynn blurs through three and four and starts his passage through the dogleg of the main straight. He declines, I note, to flick the apex as I have done. Something to remember. Wind, oil, dogleg apex, rising sun. There is much to influence these strong but twitchy Thoroughbreds.

Finally, as Wynn completes his first hot lap, One-Eye and Jean-Pierre show me their clocking sheets. As I suspected, my lap times show a quickening, slow but steady. No lap was slower than the previous until I'd reached my level, and there I stayed, like clockwork. Wynn's first lap, I know, even with cold tires and though this is a foreign track, will likely be his fastest. Here he comes through three and four again, his rear end loose, which signal is two puffs of rubber smoke from his rear tires as he works to find a straight line through the dogleg. Wynn uses up a lot of race track, always has and no doubt always will, despite contrary advice. He flashes by the pits and smiles, waves. For him, each lap's a trophy dash, a white-flag run to checkers. He's a natural, no question. Wish to God that I were, though I make no apology for my way. There are many ways to win the race.

. . .

Wynn learned to drive at One-Eye's knee four years ago—and two before me—on the whorish half-mile dirt of the Four Corners Speedway. His daddy Spencer was there as witness, as was I, not yet goaded to begin myself. They began in October, the day after the season's last race at Four Corners, and worked through cold November and raw December. One-Eye's approach, at the different times he tutored each of us, was to assume we didn't know anything about driving, which in my instance was a nearly true assumption—or about cars, which in Wynn's case was total truth.

Wynn chafed. Behind his bloodhound's face lurked a bulldog's personality: strong-willed, restless, without fear. In January he blew, and in consequence, One-Eye ventured to the wheel of a race car for the first time since before the war—he had fair promise, so he says—and the acquisition of his nickname. A false spring had blown up from the distant Gulf, and we were all in shirtsleeves. On dirt, the driving style was to power slide, and Wynn was naturally good. He'd cock the steering wheel halfway down the straight and, with the rear end broken loose, stay hard on throttle until his car was finished with the turn and pointed down the other chute. One-Eye proposed another way, less brutal to the car: stay high on the track, and at the entrance to the turn flick the wheel but once, and gently, while lifting slightly from the gas. Thus, the car could track, not slide, the measure of the turn, on a tightrope thin and delicate.

Tricky business, to be sure. Wynn worked a sweat for hours, but no results emerged. He wished to throw the car and let electric reflexes bring him round. But neither Spencer nor One-Eye would yield in their efforts, even as the bleak midwinter sun descended and a watery chill returned to harden up the air.

Wynn roared off number four and gave the wheel a mighty thrash. The car looped once, and once again.

School's out, mumbled One-Eye.

Sons of bitches, Wynn roared, sliding to a stop scant inches from where we stood. This shit is fucking impossible. Shit blueballed crap.

And so on, so forth.

One-Eye, damn, he ranted on. If you think you can do this, do. The car's broke in damned good by now, I'd say. Have at it once yourself.

I believe I will, said One-Eye.

And before he or Spencer could think the matter through, he clambered in, a one-eyed mechanic who hadn't felt the surge of racing speed in twenty years and more, goaded into showing one with half his years and twice his talent how to get through bullring worn-out rutted turns in dead of winter.

What are you doing? Spencer queried, the first to reason.

This won't take but two laps, muttered One-Eye out of Wynn's blind hearing. So I hope.

One-Eye started off, took one lap slow to gain the old sensations. Damn if the car didn't feel good. He knew the figures Wynn was staring at. Wynn's fast lap power-sliding was 23.4 seconds; his fast lap One-Eye's delicate way was 24.5: a half second's difference, and a good tip, each turn.

One-Eye's depth perception was nominal, at best. He therefore picked a marker at the entrance to each of the two wide turns, one plus two and three plus four, where he figured he'd best begin to flick the wheel and feather. In the first turn, one and two, this was a crack in the cement of the main grandstand; in the other, three and four, the marker was a fence post with a raven settled on. The raven had been there most of the afternoon, off and on. If the raven moved, One-Eye stood to lose Wynn's confidence forever, and maybe more.

The tar-black bird stayed on its roost. One-Eye hit both markers on the button, and took but one lap at speed. Before he killed the throttle and returned, having overshot the pits by only ten feet or so, he knew he'd made his point.

Wynn's bloodhound jaw was slack.

How'd I do? One-Eye ventured, striving hard to hide his shaking hands.

Twenty-two-seven, Wynn said. Fuck this shit.

Wynn picked up his jacket. His street car laid two lines of rubber blasting off.

Breaking mustangs must be easier, Spencer said.

The trick's to break the horse and not its spirit, One-Eye said with little joy.

Next day was bitter cold, the track hard-rutted, nearly turned to ice. Spencer said that through the night his son maintained glum silence, unsure whether to return. He did, though, thirty minutes late, driving through the gate atop turn one and across the track to the pits with a London cabbie's icy calm.

Car ready? he asked.

One-Eye nodded.

Clock every lap, then, he said.

One-Eye had no idea what Wynn would do next. He looked to Spencer, found no clue. Wynn took half a dozen easy warm-up laps, then floored the gas off four and half-way down the straight he cocked the wheel hard and threw his car into an old-way power slide. In three laps he had worked his way to 25 seconds flat, a time, considering the conditions, in the category of miracles. On the next lap he did the turns One-Eye's way, high and soft and straight, on rails. His sixth lap was 23.4 seconds, equal to his best the day before, his way, on a faster, smoother track. One-Eye waved him in.

How'd I do? he asked, a bloodhound's bulldog grin betraying what he knew.

You're getting the hang of it, One-Eye said.

Spencer had a lecture ready.

There're no such birds as instant heroes in this trial, he began. I don't care how good you think you are. If you went out here next spring and blew the fenders off the boys your first time out, that would only mean you'd won a race, no more—not that you knew how to drive.

The distinction was too subtle for Wynn's short grasp. But, daddy, he said. All I want to do is win the race.

. . .

I smile at such a memory. I leave One-Eye and Jean-Pierre and walk up the pit road toward the fourth turn, the better to observe this bloodhound bulldog march his paces, rear end loose and waggly. He sees me, waves again, and gestures to a high-up corner of the silver grandstand. There, to the sun, sits Annalise, bronzed and tawny, lean and lanky, pouty full-lipped Annalise. She wears short-shorts and a halter top, no more, her waist-length cinnamon-golden hair was descending.

Betsy Potter's my girl. Was my girl. Has a conscience, wishes one for me. I claim I do, and thus our terminal dispute on Wylie's past demise.

Though she must see me, Annalise declines to wave or look my way. Annalise, once Wylie's, two weeks gone, now favors Wynn, the bulldog parts, and will have nothing more to do with me or any other Mavis.

CHAPTER
6

While Annalise and I don't see even on much of anything, it's true, my feelings for her father know no bounds. If love is measured by degree of willing sacrifice, as some incline to say, then One-Eye's whom I love, for there is nothing I would not do for him, no explanation necessary. I do love that old man—not so old, maybe six or seven years older than Wylie at Wylie's demise. Nobody calls him Old Man Rivers, though, not even we when we were kids; bearing and kind dignity forbid such declination of his self.

He's a truly funny man, One-Eye, which makes my delight in him somehow all the more profound. Every now and then One-Eye finds himself confronted by a stranger low on thought.

One-Eye, you ever drive a race car? asks the stranger. I know you work on them real fine, but did you ever drive one?

Now, what kind of dumb-fool question is that? is

One-Eye's slightly false reply. Tell me the last time you ever heard of a one-eyed race-car driver. I wasn't all that good back when I had two good eyes, even on the highway.

That always draws the smile due it, and One-Eye tries to twinkle with what there's left to twinkle with, but can't. A curtain descends and masks his face in remembered agony of the accident so long ago that cost him half his eyes, and more.

The year was 1940, nearing Christmas, the last, as matters turned, before the war would find its way across the seas. Two weeks before the holiday, Mae, his wife, asked to drive to Terminus for some tinsel shopping and he said fine. He and Mae had been married but two short years, were getting to like each other real well; besides, this would be their daughter Annalise's first real Christmas.

Mae and I were married in the fall of '38, said One-Eye. Annalise waited to debut just long enough to silence wagging tongues. Not, if you know what I mean, that she couldn't have found her stage earlier than she did.

They made a day of it. Annalise, all thirteen months of bubble and cheer, was an angel, and Mae had a grand old time among the fancy ladies of Terminus, tearing through the stores like tomorrow would never come. They couldn't buy much quality, opted instead for quantity to put beneath their fresh-cut Christmas tree. They had a time, and none of the three could have been happier than then.

They left Terminus at dark. As soon as One-Eye fixed on Highway 77, the air turned cold and the rain began to thicken. The farther up they drove on the rising plain between the city and the foothills, the nastier it got. One-Eye, not yet named, heard the sleet rattle off his tin sedan. He slowed so much they weren't hardly moving. Annalise slumbered in the back seat. They had just crossed the Stokes County line, cresting a hill that on clear nights offered a twinkling view of the distant town, when Mae screamed.

One-Eye never saw the other car, but felt its presence, sliding fast and out of control, no lights, right at them. If he had seen the other car he might have flicked the wheel, driven off the road, something. Anything. As it was, all he could do was lean across Mae, crushing her fragile weight into the soft seat, before he heard the sound of Satan's banshees, and felt the bright and blinding pain.

How long he lay there he doesn't know. He was on the pavement, covered with a blanket, felt the driving sleet try to wake him up. Only he couldn't wake up. Every time he tried for consciousness, it was like in a dream where you struggle and struggle to wake up, but when you do, you find only that you're in another dream, still captured.

He drifted in and out a host of times. Everything was black, the sickly smell of blood and oil pervasive. Sometimes he heard voices, speaking low and hollow from far away, but all he felt was the cold sleet on his face, trying to wake him up.

One hollow voice was Dozier's.

Don't worry about Mae none, the sheriff said in a voice reserved for churchly sacraments. There's nothing we can do for her. Get on to Wendell, over here, and let's look on Annalise.

Then One-Eye heard his daughter's cry from up inside the shattered car. No cry of pain or even fear. Just a baby's cry.

That's when I asked the Lord to take me and leave Mae behind, said One-Eye, for the sake of Annalise. But He must have been busy elsewhere.

One-Eye was three days and nights in the hospital at

Terminus before he woke up for good and could be told the bitter truth of Mae, already known. He never even got to bury her.

Ironic, wasn't it, said One-Eye. Within the year, all the young men, boys, really, were starting off to war and coming back shot up inside and messed up in the head, or maybe not coming back at all. And I missed everything. Maybe I even came out a little bit ahead on the war, if you don't count how it came to be that I didn't go. But I do —count up everything—and there's a cancerous sadness that won't ever go away.

They fixed him up good. Unless you stare close, you wouldn't know there's a thing wrong with him. There's nothing much good about losing an eye, especially the way he lost his, though it has never hurt his poker play. More than once when he's been low and trying to bluff with a hand so flat he couldn't make a fit with a deck of wild jokers, he's reached up and popped out that right eye and placed it in the center of the table against the greenbacks and the slippery chips and the deeds to the mobile homes, and stared as hard and as mean as he can with what is left to stare with, dare and double dare. Hands fold so quick you'd think the deck was twos and threes. The other players sit with loppy peckers thinking: What *else* he gonna raise with, Billy Bob?

Oh, yes, said One-Eye, but that works best with strangers, and only once. But many's the time I think about Dozier saying not to worry about my Mae, and hearing little Annalise cry her baby's cry, and my feeling the cold sleet on my face, trying to wake me up. Maybe Annalise would have turned out a different way if she'd had her mother's hand in guidance. But maybe not. That's one of those things we never will know about, will we?

CHAPTER 7

I bounce within the fool's-gold confines of my past, and Wylie's, too . . .

One Saturday evening in the summer of my seventh year, Wylie, as had become his custom, took coffee with Heyward at Miss Dee's as final preparation for his whiskey run.

You get yourself a room tonight in Terminus, said Heyward. Here's ten for room and board, and here's directions to a place. Meet me there in early morning. There's some sport on hand I think will interest you.

Silent Wylie shrugged and made a breadcake-easy run, alone, and next day at the appointed hour drove to the appointed place in *Thunder Too*.

A barren field, it was, north of town a decent way, but a field for plowing no longer. In the center were twenty cars, all whiskey cars like Wylie's, and twenty drivers, some familiar from Miss Dee's and Terminus haunts, others strangers. Surrounding them, though this was unclear from a distance, was more or less a race track. More or less was fair description, for this track was nothing but a flattened circle in the red-clay dirt about—but not precisely, to be sure—a quarter mile around and rudely manicured. No fences bound the outside of the track; the inside dimensions were simply marked by fat and awesome-treaded tractor tires, lined in the curves to show the limits of the turns.

Somebody waved: Heyward. Others beckoned: Uncle Julian and One-Eye.

For an hour and more on that fated Sunday morning, Wylie simply sat in silence on the hood of Uncle Julian's car, a fact of presence that twitched Julian's fastidious manner. Each race lasted but ten laps and involved no more than six or eight cars, willy-nilly, so it seemed. As the morning moved toward afternoon, some drivers left and others quick replaced them.

Wylie lined up his questions and fired them one by one.

The long and short was that these were whiskey cars, no secret, owned by men like Heyward who ran the trade throughout the region. This was their sporting day. Talk and bragging over who's the fastest car had led to Sunday day-off racing. Heyward and his bootleg whiskey rivals owned the cars and raced them for their pleasure, straight and side bets on the outcome adding monetary thrill to the proceedings. It was a status thing. Jason Martin had been Heyward's driver, and Heyward had taken guff enough since Jason's sad demise. Others could have run for him, and did, but none performed as well as Jason had, and it was Uncle Julian, knowing Wylie's tripping habits more than most, who suggested bringing Wylie in.

Who pays? asked Wylie, sharply noting that these trip cars, however sturdy on Highway 77, bruised easily when bumped by others, sometimes rolling over.

Don't worry, said Heyward. That's not from your pocket, if it's racing-damaged.

And the drivers? What's the price for me?

If you win, said Heyward, the prize is twenty-five dollars paid by me. If you don't win, there's nothing to be had.

Bull to that, said Wylie. That's a fraction of the betting money.

If I win, you win, said Heyward from behind his shades. If I don't win, neither do you.

The prize you offer's half the trip money, said calculating Wylie. Why should I break my ass for you to win so little?

Because, said Heyward, a smile returning, there's a bunch of fellows who'd just love to trip for me out of Four Corners. You're reliable and pretty good, but you're not the only leadfoot chauffeur in the county. Simply put, if you don't race for me, you don't trip for me.

Julian and One-Eye listened close. Heyward was playing a bluff game, of sorts. There weren't that many who'd trip from Four Corners, and if he was going to pull a threat, he'd have done one with Uncle Julian long before. What Heyward banked on, and what he got, was Wylie's adrenaline flow. The sight of the trip cars and the track had pumped him up.

If I'm going racing, said Wylie, I'd better go.

One-Eye took control from there. First, he taped the headlights of *Thunder Too*, then tied the trunk door down with rope and with another strand attempted to strap in Wylie.

Leave it off, said gruff Wylie. I want to be able to get the hell out without being cut in two.

One-Eye shrugged. He used the rope instead to tie the

side doors shut and found a leather strap of small dimensions to wrap around the battery. And that was that.

Wylie ran some laps alone while Heyward moved among his betting friends. Soon ten cars lined up in five rows of two, in no predetermined order, and slowly trundled round the track. The car behind Wylie's tapped him once, just to let Wylie know it was there. Another lap went by in this precise formation, but off the fourth turn suddenly all the cars jumped forward, nine of ten, and were gone. Wylie, blind-started, hit the gas, but late and hard, and *Thunder Too* was sideways and every which way, and in a country second poor Wylie was over the lip of the outside of the first racing turn of his life and running through a real field.

That about pissed me off, Wylie later said. My damned hat was down around my nose and I couldn't see for shit, but the car was running still, and I just kept going around the outside of the track until I found a place to get back on it, running tenth of ten.

Heyward, One-Eye, and Julian had tears of laughter on their cheeks and stitches in their sides as Wylie wrestled.

But he finished, though lapped twice by all but one. The next race came, and Wylie volunteered the last-row slot, to watch and follow. And once again, in three and four laps' time the other cars tapped and slid him by. When Wylie looked to eyeball them, he saw the laughter in their eyes, not friendly laughter, but mean laughter coming from mean faces. And Wylie knew at that moment that Jason Martin hadn't been killed getting run empty by the *po*-lice, as all had said. That knowledge was release to Wylie. A rush came over him, made him clearheaded and see the world in a new and vigorous light.

I have to give Wylie that. All that he turned out to be was not his doing alone.

Wylie raced again that day, with similar result.

I heard sounds on *Thunder Too* I'd never heard in months of tripping, said Wylie. I thought it was going to fall apart right there in front of God and everybody. And all the damn time there were Julian and One-Eye and Heyward looking and laughing like they'd seen a cow fuck an antelope.

You did okay, said Heyward. The car isn't hurt and you're not hurt. We'll be back. You did okay.

Throughout morning and into the early afternoon maybe a couple of hundred spectators filtered in to watch, gathered in careful knots along the outside of the track. With the racing over, Wylie noticed that the drivers went through the crowd with their hats or helmets—some had tiny leather racing helmets—and the people would drop coins into the hats.

It reminded Wylie of the trampled souls he'd seen in Terminus before the war, selling apples and pencils. But Wylie wiped his face of the dust and worked the crowd with the others. He got no response until one man—by the prosperous look of him Wylie figured he was one of Heyward's whiskey buddies—threw a quarter his way. It landed short, in the dust at Wylie's feet.

Wylie let it lie there. The man beckoned for him to pick it up. Wylie spit on it and ground it deep and hard into the red dirt and walked away.

. . .

Wylie, all could tell, was bountifully enthusiastic on the cornfield race track, the location of which kept changing as it flat wore out, but from the start he was wild, erratic. Only a strong sense of self-preservation—one I hope he's

66

deeded on to me—kept him from serious harm. In all his years of whiskey racing, he ran the car into the ground and took all sorts of chances, but never hurt himself or did the damage to *Thunder Too* that One-Eye couldn't fix. Still, there was something odd about Wylie's hard and dirty driving, all agreed. He'd win his share and get his twenty-five dollars from Heyward after Heyward had collected from his bootleg betting buddies, but he'd also lose others in the strangest ways: go over the lip of the track; cut a tire. Sometimes he'd pull off the track and tell One-Eye that *Thunder Too* just wouldn't drive anymore, but when One-Eye'd take the car on back to his shop at Heyward's mill and tear it down, more often than otherwise there wouldn't be a damned thing wrong. One-Eye would turn the ignition key and *Thunder Too* would fire up and run growly-cat-like for ten minutes, while Heyward fumed and Wylie hid behind his grim, phlegmatic mask.

In the summer of my ninth year, Wylie was more and more away from home. While he still worked at Heyward's mill and tripped and whiskey-raced, instead of one night out for, say, a Saturday whiskey run and a Sunday corn-field race, he'd be gone two and three.

This went on. Near the first of August, at the worst of heat, came news that Wylie had lost *Thunder Too*.

I got run, he said when Heyward queried.

Tell how, asked Heyward, for never had brash Wylie lost a car before.

Near Madison, said Wylie. That mean-ass sheriff run me good. Couldn't catch me, but at the turn to the drop I saw a trucker's accident and suddenly there was no place to go. I had to leave the car, the load as well.

That'll cost, said Heyward.

How much?

Whatever it takes One-Eye to build you back a new one. You should be clear of me by Christmas, maybe sooner.

Which then is when Wylie suggested racing partnership.

Give me half that betting money you make off me, he said to Heyward.

Can't do that, was Heyward's walk-away response. Besides, you haven't exactly made me rich, or proud. At least Jason brought the car home.

All but once, said Wylie.

All but once.

In the middle of that selfsame August, the dog days' worst, Wylie asked One-Eye to meet him in Terminus on the sly. One-Eye complied, motoring to a small garage on the town's south side. Wylie stood out front, for the first time since his coming home a grin across his face.

He opened the garage door, and there in front was *Thunder Too*, painted red beyond the richness of even Scarlett's hair. One-Eye's jaw dropped a notch.

Heyward had his chance, said Wylie. Here's yours. There's a race track here in Terminus, as you know, a real race track. I'm going to race there, and you're my mechanic.

How long you think you can keep this quiet from Heyward? was One-Eye's numb reply.

Not long, but what can he do? One word of testimony and Heyward's through, behind the bars.

You'd do that to Heyward?

If pushed, I would. Not until.

Where's the money for this? asked One-Eye, knowing that though the car was gratis, the garage was not.

I've run three summers for that sumbitch, said Wylie. What little money there was to earn is here. I need you, One-Eye. Work on it. Turn it into a real race car for me.

Make it go fast. I can drive it. There isn't anybody who can touch us.

One-Eye, easily weakened, fell. And soon both he and Wylie were away. One-Eye filled his hours at the mill, as did Wylie. Heyward maintained silence, did not suspect, or, if he did, accuse. Indeed, One-Eye double-dutied Wylie's replacement trip car, and in mid-September of that same year Wylie again raced a whiskey race.

Nothing funny about his driving then. He started in the third row and in two laps had passed the four cars ahead of him and won without a sweat.

Heyward was delighted, until Wylie asked, How much did you make on me in that last race?

Really isn't much your business, said Heyward.

How much?

About eight hundred, reckoning loosely.

Half that's rightfully mine.

I don't think so.

You give me half, or we're through.

Then, Wylie, we are through.

Fine and good, said Wylie, his blazing eyes ablaze. Find yourself another cock to do your fighting for you.

Just might build myself a ring, said Heyward in his parting.

So. In a moment's proud fury, Heyward Scrivens lost himself a mill hand, a tripper, and a race-car driver, and soon he lost his mechanic as well. One-Eye had fallen in love with racing and saw his future clear. Neither returned to Four Corners that night or for the week. They lived in Wylie's tiny garage, borrowing two cots to sleep, and worked on *Thunder Too* until they got the former trip car near where One-Eye felt it ought to be.

CHAPTER

8

The year of '49 continued fortuitous well into brisk October. Whiskey racing neared its end, giving way to real race tracks, such as the one where now I walk and wander, dreaming of things I never saw or heard and waiting to fulfill my destiny. No, not this glistening, nearly virgin superspeedway, paved and railed all around, but rather its rude predecessor.

The Terminus Speedway—the old Terminus Speedway—was dirt, of course, and dusty, a mile around and fast; an easy track to drive—all is relative—but deadly once the error was made. The shows were occasional Thursday nights beneath dim-dusty lights, or Sunday afternoons, the starting time placed forward to salve the wrath of Sabbath Christians.

Wylie debuted there three weeks beyond his dissolution from Heyward. The program called for formal qualifications—one car at a time in stopwatch trial—to be followed by four ten-lap heat races and a consolation spurt for losers low and slow. Next there was a semi-main of maybe twenty-five laps to flesh out the card, and finally a main event of forty laps, no more.

Wylie was a quick study, and One-Eye, too. Whiskey cars and whiskey racing were unforgiving tutors. Both men took their instruction with hard intent, observed how others drove and tweaked their cars, did homework to improve. Wylie was spectacular in his Terminus debut. He qualified sixth fastest and won a heat, and in the semi-main, coincidence, or fate, or call it what you will, put him in the starting line directly ahead of a burnt-orange car of such immaculate preparation that even One-Eye, no slouch for cleanliness and detail, turned in admiration.

A pretty car, he said to Wylie. It's not run whiskey, that's a bet. It's built for racing, nothing more.

It's fast and quick, said Wylie. The driver knows his way around.

As Wylie soon found out. The other car gave Wylie trouble from the outset, jumped him on the start, and cleanly moved ahead, a trick that fuming Wylie quick made note of. Wylie, faster in the trials, tried to pass his sudden rival back. He bumped the other in the rear; the other held its ground. He tried to pass up high; the other moved up half a racing groove to give the choice of running into it or bouncing off the guard rail. He tried the other low, nuzzling his front to push the burnt-orange other up and out—this, too, without result. The other car held firm and steady, so much so that Wylie later said he thought the damned thing had to be cement.

This way and that, they darted and jabbed. To One-Eye, it was a pretty sight, and deep down a tinge of disappointment settled when the checkers for the semi-main brought end to such a jousting combat.

Wylie had other thoughts.

71

Who is that bastard? he shouted at One-Eye even before he'd cut the switch.

One-Eye scampered out to see. He returned in shortened time with double news.

The fellow's name is Spencer Tatum, he said. He's been racing here the year the track's been open. And you'd never guess who's standing by his car.

So tell me. I'm in no mood for question games.

Heyward Scrivens.

. . .

Racing's full of melodrama, little question of that. Coincidence abounds, the stars line straight, the fates contrive to add adventure to a common day. In the main event that afternoon—forty laps, thus forty miles of dusty, sliding racing—Wylie and Spencer once again made introductions to each other. Not for fourth place as had been the earlier case—one not of awesome import—but for first.

Both their cars were working fine, said One-Eye. Once they'd passed the cars in front of them, you knew they'd be racing to the flag.

Assuming, of course, they made it to the flag, an issue soon in doubt.

Damn, Wylie worked him over. Spencer was first and Wylie second, and Wylie tried every whiskey trick he knew to gain the lead. High, low, dash, dart, push, nudge —it was the semi-main all over again, and the fans, who knew a brabble in the making, stood to cheer its onset.

This went on for an ancient time, but Spencer, equally fast and more experienced, held him off, held him off, until one fateful passage halfway through.

Spencer had the outside line, and Wylie, once again, dipped down half a groove as the two cars fled along the front straight to turn one. Wylie dipped another half a groove, and this time pulled nearly even with Spencer, but not quite. The pass was started, but not sufficiently made when time came for both to turn. All agreed the right-of-way was clearly Spencer's—but one.

Wylie didn't yield. He stayed his course, straight-lined for the first turn's guard rail, long past the well-marked point where he should have called retreat. Suddenly the realization was Spencer's that they were engaged in a deathly game of chicken, and that Wylie, simply put, was not going to lift. The choice of what to do was Spencer's. His decision controlled their relationship, and the relationship between all Mavises and all Tatums, from that dread moment ever forward.

Spencer lifted, let relentless Wylie go.

The grandstand cheered. The fans stood and waved their hats when next the two cars sallied down the front. Spencer didn't give Wylie the race for free after that. He stayed on Wylie's bumper and made him work to keep his ill-got gain. A poet might have rhymed the justice that followed. Five laps from the end, Wylie popped a tire, in part, no doubt, from Spencer's worrying him so hard. Wylie held the car firm and coasted to a back-straight stop while all the others, Spencer foremost, passed him to the flag and money.

Wylie should have been pleased enough with his maiden race-track run, but no. Spencer ventured to Wylie's pit soon after, to offer introductions all around.

Tough luck, Wylie, Spencer said. Let me stand you to a beer.

You took your sweet time lifting for me, is what Wylie said.

Huh?

Back there when I drove under you and passed, you

waited awfully long to let me go. I thought you might have half a mind to chop me. Try that again and I'll knock you in the toolies.

Mavis, Spencer said, you got away with something that could have wrecked two fine race cars and maybe more. I'm not big on revenge, but if you don't cool your head, there's gonna be somebody down the road who'll get you back if you keep pulling this shit.

You knocked me around pretty good yourself.

You gave as good as you got. I haven't seen you here before, but I know your name. I suspect you'll be around.

Suspect so, said Wylie.

The beer's still yours, for you and One-Eye, if you'll take the offer.

Before Wylie could respond, up walked Heyward. He nodded to Spencer, then to Wylie and One-Eye, and walked measured circles around what all knew was *Thunder Too*: one tire flattened, its once-fire-red sheen reduced by dust and oil to muddied disrepute. *Thunder Too* and driver, crew were a less than noble sight.

Nice car you got there, fellas, Heyward said. None could see his eyes, but the rest of him looked grim.

Not bad, thanks, said One-Eye.

You fellas make much money today?

Neither Wylie nor One-Eye ventured the obvious answer.

I'll keep the mill jobs open for you fellas, said Heyward. You just call when the money runs out, hear? . . . And by-the-by—I thought you'd like to know—I've had a talk with Spencer here, and he's agreed with my suggestion to move his racing operation up to Four Corners. Maybe open up a garage to do some work for me.

I'll be up when the racing's done this year. Spencer nodded by way of confirmation.

And so it came that gentle Spencer, bloodhound Wynn, and wifely mother Mary moved into our orb, outsiders of a sort, though quickly taken in—a grace occurrence due more to Tatum pliancy than Mavis welcome courtesy.

CHAPTER

9

So tawny Annalise won't wave. Screw her. Betsy Potter's my lady; was. I study Wynn in turn four and add a mental note to my filling storage. There's a nasty dip and bump that's posted squarely in the middle of the groove, at the point where the car slides almost to the outside rail before it straightens for the straight. I have chosen to straddle the bump, an easy business alone but one that offers trickery in traffic. Wynn declines evasion. He angles for the dippenbump on purpose. When his car is lightened by the catapult effect, he flicks the wheel a sharp one. When the car settles back—bravo!—it's pointed straight, the turn negotiated clean.

Wynn's trial's through. Like me, he unhooks himself while Bent Nose and Red Face take tire temperatures and One-Eye and Jean-Pierre confer. We break for lunch, wolfing steamy hot plates at a nearby diner. The talk's diffused, not on the subject of our trial. I study Andriotti, an easy man to be around despite his power and prestige.

So brilliant was his racing star that he could have had his pick of cushy jobs with European industry upon retirement. Instead, he claimed a fascination with Detroit.

Any fool can build *one* car to run five hundred miles at a racing speed, he's fond of saying. Detroit's great trick is building millions to last a hundred thousand miles at sixty miles per hour.

Silver-haired and slight, he has a soft and friendly presence that belies his power to anoint a driver with the portent of greatness by a simple yes or no, a judicious exercise that has not left him unscathed in his middle-fifty years. Otherwise patrician, he drinks milk on ice and that alone, and all ten nails on his delicate fingers are bloodied, raw, chewed downward to the quick.

Nerves, he says. Driving race cars cost me my stomach; managing a factory racing team has cost me my cuticles.

In mid-afternoon, beneath a sun now hazed and lowering, we return to the race track. On instructions from Andriotti, we are told our solo runs are through and now we'll run together.

No racing, says Andriotti. This is not a contest for the flag. Run the cars together. Find out how they like each other.

The black boxes remain. Though now the race cars are paramount, and they alone, I note the sensors still are hooked to man and car alike. This trial remains a double billing, still.

We fire up. Once again, the soothing grumbles emanate from underneath, it seems, our iron beasts. Before we leave the pits, Wynn nudges his car forward and profoundly taps me on my rear bumper, a sound I feel more than hear beneath the engines' roar.

Bent Nose's nose is misshapen by this.

Watch that shit, he mouths in our direction. These cars aren't yours, yet.

I succeed in looking stern, though blood drips from where I bite my tongue. I can't judge Wynn's mood. Tinted sun goggles—I have none—hide from me his present coloration. One-Eye squinches up his nose in mock alarm; Jean-Pierre looks the other way. We roll on out.

      . . .

We were inseparable, Wynn and I, from the beginning, and I guess Annalise, too, until she got too girlish for our tastes. Mainly, it was Wynn and I, with Wynn the leader and I the follower, no matter that I out-aged him by nine months, a full school year. I sure didn't outsize him, though, and I, no voluntary fighter, knew my place in the pugilistic order.

When I first met him, Wynn was a friendly blob, a freckled red tomato, until he lost his fat and turned into a brick. Despite his size and early misshape, Wynn always had the lithe coordination of a bobcat. A natural jock, and lucky that, for his curiosity of the world was nil, or of how the world turned. Ironic, being Spencer's son, but how things worked—a toy, a toaster—intrigued him not. He disassembled well enough, but I never knew him to put the thing together again.

I was just the opposite, and this, perhaps, was cause of our attraction. Where Wynn was large and strong, I was small and spindly: One-Eye once said he figured I'd been put together with an Erector set, or Tinkertoys. Where Wynn was open and accepting, I existed by myself, except when I chose otherwise. Where Wynn showed little inclination to ask the how of things, my curiosity was fierce and tenacious. However quietly my queries led me, they led me nonetheless. Still, I was follower and Wynn was leader, a satisfaction to both our younger, rough-formed selves.

Wynn, the bumptious leader; I, the cautious follower, though never shy of trying. North of town there was a special creek, and near the county line a natural swimming hole. On the far bank was a spreading, sprawling live-oak tree. At first reconnaissance, Wynn scampered up the tree a limb and, caution to the winds, dived in. Emerging triumphant, he climbed a higher branch and dived again. I paddled in the pool, measuring the depth and breadth of it. Satisfied of all dimensions, I, too, joined in the contest. A higher limb for me, and then for Wynn, and then for me—an even contest of hard wills and granite nerves. What swayed the balance was Wynn's hefty bulk and my lack thereof.

Wynn finally couldn't climb a higher branch. I could, and did, peering intensely at the murky water now far far far below my swaying perch. Having proved my point, I descended to the notch where Wynn had last plunged in, and jumped from there.

Or snakes. Black snakes and king snakes abounded in the county, and an occasional lost copperhead, nothing more. But once we heard the rumor that a farmer'd seen a big old thick timber rattler. Unlikely as the sighting was, Wynn insisted we set out in hot pursuit, and damn us both if we didn't find it—or one that fit the broad description. It was on a narrow trail through the fields near the farmer's barn. It was thick, all right. It looked to be four inches around and six feet long and had a good dozen rattles. Old snake. Mean snake. But asleep snake, sunning itself coiled like a fire hose.

Now what? I murmured so as not to wake it.

I dunno, said Wynn. Never thought about what we'd do if we caught it. Never thought we'd catch it.

We haven't exactly caught it yet, I pointed out.

Wynn ran off to get a burlap bag. I found a dead branch with a Y-shaped end like a frog gigger. We edged closer.

If you miss, I'm running, said Wynn.

You got us here, I said. I'm not gonna miss.

I didn't. Wynn carried the bag back to One-Eye's mill garage.

Got that snake, I said.

Uh-huh, One-Eye said.

We did, said Wynn.

Wynn walked outside and set down the prize. In a nickel flash the snake emerged. It wasn't coiled, and it moved like fury. Whereupon I gigged it again.

Whereupon One-Eye ambled inside his shop, emerged with a double-bladed ax, and guillotined our catch.

I bounce ahead, my mind lazy, melancholy . . .

· · ·

Early one September Sunday morning in the summer of my fourteenth year, I awoke to the sound of thrown pebbles against my bedroom window. Shivering in the chill, I looked down and out to see Wynn standing, begging silence.

Get dressed, he whispered. C'mon.

I complied with some reluctance. Even then, given a choice, my day would not begin till noon.

What's up? I queried.

Going for a ride, said Wynn. I borrowed the car for a couple of hours. Get yours.

Borrow was not the exact word. While Spencer and

Mary didn't object too heartily to Wynn's use of their family car, neither were they often consulted. The unsaid attitude seemed to be that if Wynn and car returned intact, then nothing would be said. While often a passenger on these shady rides, this was the first time the suggestion had come to find wheels of my own.

Our car? My car? squeaked incredulous I. You're nuts. I can't. Wylie'll kayo me.

He's pooped from racing last night, said Wynn, who'd been.

I hadn't, rarely did go, then. But I knew he'd cut a tire qualifying, crashed in his heat, and had to bend out a lot of sheet metal before the main, then wrestle an ill-handling car for forty laps with no possibility of a high finish.

No keys, I said with less conviction.

No need.

Wynn had parked the Tatums' Chevrolet, a brand-new '55 V-8, two blocks away. Wylie's Ford was directly in front of our house. Wynn took a thin metal band the size of a ruler, slipped it down the window, and jiggled. Up popped the lock button.

Oh shit, I said, a measure of my acquiescence.

You steer, said Wynn. I'll push.

I slipped behind the wheel, the door open, my left foot on the ground for added leverage, and committed. We pushed the car to where Wynn's was parked. Wynn raised the hood and tinkered with the innards; similarly, then, inside beneath the dashboard. I was silent, let the giddy flush of guilt wash over me. At Wynn's command, I again got behind the wheel, depressed the clutch, and heard the starter motor turn, a sound as shattering as any I'd experienced.

Wynn slammed shut my door with a coffin's-lid finality. In a moment, we were off, slow and silent down Stokes Boulevard until we reached the eastern limit of the town. Wynn easily built his speed and I followed. We headed directly into the morning sun, whose clear and cool light promised to bathe the day in glory.

We drove, running easily, for miles and miles on the empty country roads that wound through thin valleys and twisted round gentle hillocks. The tires sang on the smooth dark narrow asphalt.

Wynn slowed, motioned me ahead. I pulled to go around, but when our cars were even, Wynn bumped his speed. We ran this way until a blind curve forced me back in line. Beyond the turn, a startled farmer atop an oncoming tractor waved in greeting.

Again Wynn slowed and I pulled out; again Wynn challenged my right of passage. I slipped behind him, let him slow. With sudden acceleration I tried to shoot on by, but he, anticipating, blocked my lane. I flicked back to the right lane, edging to within a half car's length of even. Wynn forced me to the shoulder.

Then Wynn slowed to nothing and let me by. Our roles reversed, now I declined to let him by. But at a certain sweeping left turn down the road, Wynn pulled beside me in the oncoming lane, waved, and smiled. Likewise, I.

I eased into the turn. Before I could comprehend, we bumped, and in a moment both flew straight off the road and through a one-strand-barbed-wire fence, smack to the middle of a grassy pasture, tabletop smooth, still heavy with the morning's dew.

You son of a bitch, I mumbled, contemplating the dent in the left-front fender of Wylie's pristine Ford.

This is great, said Wynn, ignoring my lament.

What's great? Wylie's gonna shoot me.

Maybe later. Teach you to keep your eyes open. I knew what I was doing.

Send me a telegram, I muttered.

Wynn drove alone to the far end of the pasture, turned around, and headed back directly for my Ford. At a goodly rate of speed. I was ready to leap when Wynn cocked the wheel and jammed the emergency brake, and to my astonished eyes the little Chevrolet turned 180 degrees practically in its own tracks. It was a slightly wobbly whiskey turn, designed for a quick change of direction in the face of a roadblock, and I was properly impressed.

Next time by, Wynn's mark was a 360-degree rotation, maintaining his speed throughout.

Who taught you that?

Daddy, a little, said Wynn. He lets me ride with him at the races before practice starts, sometimes. The first time he done a 180, on purpose—there's a lot done not on purpose—I damned near wet my pants. The second time, I asked daddy to show me how.

We cut doughnuts on the greengrass for an hour, Wynn and I, though at first I had my trouble bringing all the car around. But in my time I got the hang and soon was popping the brake and flicking the wheel at just the moment to let the car's rear end come round as far as I wanted it to go, and when. On the dew-heavy grass the sport was easy, relatively.

You ever do this on the highway? I asked.

Not yet, said Wynn. I'm close, though. Been working hard.

My anxiety rose with the sun, and soon we took our leave. We drove slowly. Wynn's thoughts I couldn't fathom. I, subdued, was overwhelmed by sadness when we left that uncorrupted place. I tried in desperate ways to freeze the freedom and the joy of those minutes, though sensing that each following memory of the day, no matter how creative the reinvention, would be diminished from the day itself.

Five, six, maybe ten miles from Colonel Stokes, we raced again, not the playful taunting of the outward trip, but fiercer, grimmer.

Wynn, of course, started; I, of course, acquiesced.

It wasn't a bad little race, once I got the spirit of the thing. We ran even, side by side through all but the most blind of turns, and I, at least, rejoiced in those brief desperate feelings that told of risky challenge squarely faced and fairly bested.

So there we were, Wynn to my right now, I in the oncoming lane, when he tapped me. I started at the sudden, unexpected jolt. He bumped me again. This time there could be no mistaking his intent. Once might be an accident; twice was definite provocation.

My juices flowed on several fronts, most visibly the thought of Wylie's actions on our return. I could have avoided Wynn, of course, and yielded, but did not. Again, the cars clanged, hanging together in brief metallic embrace.

I faced a choice. A choice of what was certainly an unclear thought, but no less real for its shapelessness. Tears boiled up and spilled. With no informed intent, I swerved away from Wynn to the left shoulder, and then sharp right, catching Wynn's Chevrolet an unsuspected blow that knocked it mildly off its course.

I caught the startled tension in Wynn's eye. He grinned. And retaliated in kind. Our speed soon slowed.

We took to the opposite shoulders at the same time and charged back to the center of the road with percussive whangs and bangs. We switched positions to wreak our havoc—the boundary of reasonable explanation long since passed—on the cars' nether sides. By the time we reached Four Corners, neither could hardly move. Wynn's spewed steam, evidence of a busted radiator. Its right-front fender lay peeled back. First estimates from my Ford were two flat tires, a sprung hood and trunk. We made it to the statue in the center of the square, where the cars by mutual consent expired. We both emerged and stood to survey, teary-eyed, but now from laughter, as some early, unofficial coffee hounds from Miss Dee's poured out to see the ruction.

God Almighty, said Billy Winslow in rare profanity.

Dozier McCartle walked round the steaming, crumpled cars full three times three before he uttered anything, and then only a low, long whistle.

You boys all right? asked Heyward Scrivens.

We assured him we were.

That's too bad, he said, because I'd guess neither of you has got more than fifteen, twenty minutes of the good life left. What happened, hey?

Aw, hell, said Wynn. We just got into it a little.

More'n a little, I'd say, said Dozier.

Daddy and One-Eye can fix these cars up in no time, said Wynn with hope and optimism as a trail of oil crept from beneath his car.

My mind was blank in contemplation of my future.

From the opposite ends of Stokes Boulevard, two figures walked slowly to the square. Spencer wore a base-ball cap high up on his forehead and had what might have passed for a smile on his face. I knew Wynn was off the hook.

The other was Wylie.

That day's breakfast was late and quiet. Wylie and I had pushed the car home, in silence, and with Miss Ma we sat at the kitchen table feigning heavy interest in her scrambled eggs. The only sounds were the dull clicks of silverware on china, and the smacking of lips.

Not mine, however.

Isn't anybody going to say anything? I finally asked, my plate untouched, my appetite lost on a country road.

What's to say, son? asked Wylie in a rare paternal retort. You took a perfectly good, almost new car and tore it up. What for?

I told him as best I could, which wasn't much.

We were driving, I said. Wynn got pushy. I got pushy back.

Some push, said Miss Ma.

We weren't trying to hurt each other, I said (though to myself I'd asked the question). Once it got started, there didn't seem to be a way to stop.

You could have backed off, said Miss Ma. Wynn doesn't have the good sense of a milk cow, but I expect more from you. You could have yielded the way.

Wylie, to my mild surprise, turned on Miss Ma.

There's a time to stand and one to run, he said. Maybe the boy knows the difference.

I could have stopped it, I said, more to Wylie than to Miss Ma, but there didn't seem to be a way. And after a while there didn't seem to be any point.

How was the car handling? asked Wylie.

Huh?

When you were turning doughnuts and racing—before you got into the foolery—how was the car handling? You have trouble getting the car where you wanted it to go?

I think it was pushing a little, I said. It wouldn't turn as much as I wanted it to. Had to get belligerent with the steering wheel sometimes.

More silence draped the kitchen. Miss Ma cleared the table, made an undue clatter at the sink.

You'll have to pay for it, said Wylie. You'll have to work it off.

Fair, I said. How?

Check with One-Eye. He might be looking for some help.

Racing's almost over for the year.

There's always next, said Wylie. And there's the mess in front. You won't be lacking for things to do.

· · ·

Dead Wylie softens at the edges; blurs . . .

Engines warmed, we play, a half a lap apart. Wynn enters three as I find one, and exits four as I leave two. We fire down our separate straightaways, the waving, dancing dogwoods always intervening. From the pits, One-Eye counts the laps and Jean-Pierre clicks the seconds, and via Bent Nose and a blackboard, this latter information is relayed to the track. I note with glumness after several laps that Wynn is gaining. I strain for speed. Finding none more, I decline to keep my distance. I let him close until no more than one football field's length removes one car from the other. The suck does all the rest. Wynn enters the swirling partial vacuum behind my car, and when he does, the enveloping air brings him closer, closer, closer.

He rides behind me now, scant feet behind and one

half racing groove below, and we are joined again. For-ever? We ride this way for laps and laps, until he swings by me on a slingshot and I nudge up on him. We switch again. Our lap times, Bent Nose shows on chalky board, decline.

A final time Wynn draws close to my bumper. This time he stays directly behind me through three and four, and once over the humpy bump in four he fills my rearview mirror, waves casually, and slams me in the rear, no gentle tap. I am not caught unaware. This move's been done by others, when two cars are a perfect match—front bumper of one beneath the rear bumper of the other—as in fact the Dorsens are: snout-nosed iron beasts with ducktailed asses. Wynn tucks in thus and pushes me down the straight.

So engaged, we sail; both cars faster than alone, and looser. The ride this way is smoother and slipperier, slow undulating movements side to side as the mated pair of cars becomes a thing entirely new from its separate, equal parts.

I am totally at Wynn's mercy this way. He controls, pushing me from behind; I am merely a passenger whose hand happens to be at the tiller. He cannot push me through the turn this way. We must disengage and reassume our liaison twice per lap. The moment of disengagement is crucial: too soon and we lose precious ticks on Jean-Pierre's demanding watches; too late and I am dangerously high on the track.

Wynn so pushes me into turn one a fraction deep. None save Wynn or I could notice, but a fraction deep it is and I wave him off. He lets me go. The next time by, again as one, he pushes me in even deeper despite my wave, more concentrated now.

Finally, third time in, I've had enough. I dance through one and two and lift.

Wynn shoots by low as I fumble with the virgin marbles high on the track. I'm not so occupied that I can't give Wynn the finger. It's my turn now to kiss him in the ass.

PART TWO

CHAPTER 10

The sun's at work. Oil bleeds from the black and nearly virgin asphalt, pushing the racing groove up and up the track. The car still slightly understeers, but the push is not nearly as defiant as before. Bent Nose and Red Face have done their work well, at my suggestion and Jean-Pierre's command. They've screwed down one spring, loosened up another; nothing more. The car's now close to where it ought to be, for me, though not yet perfect. One more tweak of the wrench will do the trick. But not too much. The best cars are the easiest to drive when dialed in, but, in serious compensation, the devil to manage when they're not.

Wynn declined to change suspension settings at the noontime break. Probably wouldn't know the how of it, or even how to ask. While things mechanical aren't his forte, I must admit the boy can drive. My voluntary withdrawal from our little fray has cost me half a straightaway. My juices pump, fueled hard by his relentless jab at me the moment past. I give a furious chase, determined to regain the slight measure of advantage that I've yielded. I draw nearer still until I feel the turbulence of the churning air behind Wynn's car, the signal that I've caught his vacuum. The rest is a piece of cake.

Slowly, I reel him in. There's nothing he can do. Our cars are even. It's like playing with a fish you haven't quite decided yet to keep; he's yours to land or dangle, as you choose. Similarly, I close on Wynn, but at a schedule of my choosing, and plan my pass, an exercise I know will be a lap-long chore when once I start. Adding to my rectitude is my awareness that I've never passed a car on this particular track before, in earnest—what we did some minutes past was swap positions, nothing more—and Wynn, though having notched a shaky pass of me, never has himself been overtaken. To pass in entrance to the turns invites disaster. The track's too narrow all around, but in the turns the racing groove—the place where cars at teeter-totter speed *must* be—is lesser still. The choice is down to exits, out of two, or four. Not two, for there the pendulum momentum of the overtaking car cannot be lessened in time to miss the back-straight outside wall. The choice, then, is no choice at all. The exit off of four must be the place: slide carefully to the humpy bump, then twitch the car hard left and chop the turn and beat my rival to the dogleg apex, depending on the other car to yield the space when once I take the inside line for mine.

I bounce the apex, once again the red dust in arrears to indicate my left-side wheels have found a speedy line on dirt below the oily asphalt. I must be digging quite a hole by now. A second beyond, I flash by One-Eye and Jean-Pierre. One-Eye, with his chalkboard, waves me in. I wave him off and point ahead toward Wynn, now meager yards ahead of me. I am solidly in his draft now, can feel my car's gentle yaw as we move together toward turn one. I could jam him in the rear as he's done me. I know his rearview mirror is filling with my sight. A ventured finger wave of mine draws no response. I drop off one groove low and feint a low-side pass off two. He binds his car, moves off the rail to stay in front and block the place he thinks I've chosen for my overtake.

Thus, we negotiate two and fly the back chute. Again, I close him up, directly tucked, mere inches separating our mating pair of sharky Dorsens, and this way enter three. My concentration now is absolute. I watch no dials, see no heaving dogwoods in the briskly wind, think no thoughts of tawny Annalise or kindly One-Eye or fortnight-buried Wylie. In this moment of flight my mind's a blank. No thoughts of any sort intrude, save one: to stay my course and pass my rival back.

We enter three embraced. Wynn's fallen for the low-side feint I've hinted at off two and fights to hold his car in the middle of the track to block me down below. I accept his gesture with an inward smile, and midway through the three and four drift up the gentle banking so that now I'm half a car's length highside. Wynn can't block me both ways, high and low. He must make a choice and hope it's also mine. He knows, and I, I've got the power to pass. The question's where. I know the answer; he must guess.

Through three and into four. We are perfectly aligned. Wynn's bluffed. My pass is done. Now all I have to do is make it. We near the exit humpy bump. Wynn, lower than he's been all day, misses it entirely. I, higher than I've ever been, feel the car settle in the slight depression, climb the other side, and lighten. Perfect. When my car has lost totality of weight, I'll crank the wheel left and chop the turn.

The car rises. My stomach sinks, biliously, as it would atop a roller coaster's crest. The car starts its settling, and as it does I crank the wheel left—and hear, then feel, a muffled, sudden *BANG!* My car veers forward right. The steering wheel is all but wrenched from my hands. I grab it back and throw it hard to left, but positive results are not forthcoming.

Oh, good God damn, I yell.

I've blown a tire, I know. Popped the bastard all to hell. What else? Wish I could back this thing up about ten seconds. But no, the car is gone. It moves at racing speed for the outside rail, milliseconds distant.

A third time I yank the wheel, desperate, now, to reduce the angle of what I know with awful certitude will be a bang-up mess. The car has pivoted hard to right. I look straight ahead, not down the race track as before, but into the grandstand, aluminum bright and silvery-still.

I have no time to guard myself—not even close my eyes—before I strike the rail a fearsome blow. I see the rail bend and yield. Will it break? My hood springs high. No forward vision. There's a strangely comforting pain, like I've been whambellied by a monster sledge, as I lurch forward against my belt and harness.

How bad?

My wind whooshes out, a collapsing bellow of pain. My right hand slips the tacky steering wheel and slams against the toggles on the dashboard. I slide forward, caught by my crotch strap. My balls squish against the strap. Streams of fiery agony fire into my groin.

How bad?

My car begins to climb—*aah, whoo-boy*—and the metal-on-metal grating fills my ears as the car rises to the top of the shattered, shattering guard rail. Like this, we ride for hours, days, it seems. Again, I turn the steering wheel left, but the ease with which I can informs me that my car's no longer on the ground. To the left of me and three feet down, the track awaits; to the right of me, an empty parking lot, twenty feet below. I count the seconds, but what is time? Still, I count—*one*, *two*, *three*—as my car teeters and totters atop the rail, still traveling at a goodly rate of speed.

How bad?

I teeter near the track. I totter nearly out . . .

CHAPTER
11

My memory wanders through the warps of time, expanding and contracting, turning back upon itself with lazy disregard for rhyme or reason. I fix now upon a touchstone formulation of my quiet, drifting childhood. Though racing came to permeate all corners of my youthful world, I will not say it held much fascination for my youngest self. Wylie, naming one, found in this a cause for sullen anger and confusion, but my indifference would not be bent. All changed as I neared ten, the year the century reached its midpoint, when Heyward Scrivens found he had a cash-flow problem, though not the ordinary kind.

He had too much of it, not from his mill but rather from the whiskey trade, and there was just so much that he could spend without attracting notice of the wrong authorities. Some he put into the mill and some with banks, and some he gave to Dozier for keeping at the jailhouse. But Dozier, always younger than his halfway brother, got the nervous jitters with the greenback watch in direct proportion to its build-up.

And the more nervous you get, said Heyward to his sheriff brother, the more nervous I get.

I'd rather have to oversee the meanest killer in the state than worry on your money, Dozier said in his response. Nobody could take a killer from me, but one fine day the wrong soul's going to hear about that money and it's gone, even if I were to stuff it in the pillow beneath my head. It's a bad business, having money loose about. Causes an assortment of contrary reactions among a certain class of folks.

Thus did Heyward in his head sum up the ifs and wherefores of a race track of his own, and find the totals positive. He had ten fallow acres by the mill, a location he deemed perfect: close to him and close to town and hard by Highway double-seven. The red-clay land, he figured rightly, could have no better use. The stuff would break a tiller's back and soul more quickly than a locust plague.

You work that soil, Heyward said, and then you work it more. But when you're done, you're left with what you started with. Red clay doesn't change.

And so, a moment after final frost, a day in latest March when all began to bud and turn to green, Heyward Scrivens started up on what would soon become Four Corners Speedway. He drew his plans, like all of Heyward's doing after careful study only, then surveyed a flattened circle of one half mile's circumference. Next, he rented an earth grader in Terminus and got One-Eye to haul it up. One-Eye didn't work direct for Heyward anymore, but they were still on social terms, which, it should be said, was not the case with him and Wylie.

The distance chosen was a studied picking.

Lots of tracks I've seen, he said, aren't but a quarter mile and even less. But those aren't fun to watch, or drive. In five laps, no more and often less, the lead cars and the donkeys are so mixed you've no idea who's where. A mile track, like Terminus, is just too big. And fast. A race track of that proportion is faster than the cars that race it; the drivers can't keep up. A half-mile ring's the perfect compromise.

Heyward dug the infield out and moved the tons of earth outside the front straight, creating a natural embankment for his grandstand. He hoed the infield drainage trenches, laid the pipes, and then began to work the whorish racing surface. The straights were flat, but in the turns he piled earth to give a gentle banking of a few degrees—seven or eight, he figured with his eyeball.

Now was the summer heat of June. For two months after, Heyward manicured the racing surface with a gardener's patient care. He cut the clay with a spike-tooth drag, then smoothed the clay with heavy rollers, ballasted with cement. He laid on bags and bags of powdered calcium to keep in all the dust. He showered the track with water to keep down all the calcium. Then he'd spike-tooth drag it once again and roll it smooth. Twice a week he did this: drag, roll, calcium, water; drag, roll, calcium, water. And then the calendar struck August 1.

At first there was only Heyward. He tooled round and round his race track in a pickup to buffer in the surface. Others joined him. One-Eye, Wylie, Spencer—anyone who wanted to, got in his car or truck and rode around for hours, manicuring the rude red clay. The fellows from the mill joined in at casual hours, and even people from the town, driving fast or slow and high or low. Between the joyride chauffeurs, Heyward dragged and rolled, laid calcium and watered, and as the month turned dog-days still, it began to happen. The race track reached the point where when the cars and trucks buffed off the loose stuff on the top, the underneath stayed hard and firm as asphalt. The track was dry-slick seasoned, hard, and ready for a race.

Heyward's effort was but one of many. Throughout the state and region similar adventures sprouted up, and by the time of which I speak, a rude red bullring could be found no more than fifty miles' drive from any single place. The likes of Wylie, Spencer, and One-Eye, by choosing —and they did—raced as often as they liked, the frequency determined only by racing luck and iron constitution. Each track was different. Some were dusty, others strewn with stone, and others yet, through slipshod maintenance, were potholed, crumbling survival tests, no more. But every track, however slick or crude, depended for success on local heroes, home-town drivers born to bear the local colors against outlanders from afar.

Heyward had himself a pair, in Spencer Tatum and Wylie Mavis, who, despite their polar temperaments, seemed to be good buddies.

For reasons which I never understood, said Heyward. But no matter. Spencer was a gentleman; not so Wylie. He was after money—mine—and he also wanted nothing more than to strut his stuff before Miss Ma and the others in the town. Let him and Spencer win some races. That was fine. They'd bring me more in gate receipts than ever I would pay them from the purse.

And Heyward, who never left a paper trail and kept all records in his head, had not forgotten *Thunder Too*, though never once did he bring that little matter to Wylie's face, or One-Eye's either.

• • •

Heyward put down the first-ever Four Corners 100 for the second Sunday in September. He and Dozier, mainly, laced the county with posters and advertised in the *Stokes County Monitor* and even in the big daily paper down in Terminus. When he wasn't manicuring his track, he moved through the countryside, going to the other race tracks nearby and signing up the drivers. Ten days before the race, he took a full page in the *Monitor* to announce a bombshell: Rex Harding had agreed to run. That was a coup of giant proportions, and the reason wasn't hard to understand.

Rex Harding was the most famous race-car driver in the country. He was from somewhere in Ohio, and every flag-filled Memorial Day, the whole country listened on the radio to find out what he would do to lose another Indianapolis 500, the most fabulous automobile race in the world. He was a hard-luck driver if ever there was, the stuff of legends in his very own time. If there was a race he hadn't led, I never knew; if there was a major race he'd won, I was unaware of that, as well. He didn't leave a race quietly —just pull in the pits and walk off into the sunset. He'd crash, spectacularly, and the closer to the end of the race, the more appropriate it seemed to be. If the Indianapolis 500 had been the Indianapolis 450, he would have won a half dozen, before the war and after. His cars were dressed in black, a ghost of midnight chasing rainbows. The first year I remember of him, huddled in my room to dream alone, he blew a tire on the last turn of the very last lap, and one hundred thousand people stood and cried. Through the crackling static I could hear their tears. Another year he lapped the field, and then his engine blew. In this year of 1950, he was running away again when, freakishly, a wheel cracked and he tumbled down the main straight. He wasn't hurt—he had never so much as even scratched his entire career—and once again made all the headlines, not the winner.

How Rex Harding came to race at the Four Corners Speedway was testament to Heyward's diligence. He found that Harding had some family in nearby Madison and once a year, in mid-September, would amble south to hunt and fish. Finding all this out, Heyward simply paid Harding five hundred dollars to take a busman's holiday, then asked One-Eye to build an Indy hero's car, a duplicate of Wylie's *Thunder Too*.

Wylie, no surprise, had stirred emotions at this latter news.

What you gonna do? he asked of One-Eye. Build that Yankee a car so he can take our money, yours and mine?

Harding's a great race-car driver, One-Eye mollified, but he hasn't raced the dirt in six months, and he hasn't driven cars like this in five years. He won't show you up unless you let him.

Wylie grunted, reluctantly agreed. For all his posturing, Wylie was as much in awe of Harding as all others. Besides, he saw the point of One-Eye's case.

From the moment Rex Harding walked into the Speedway's loud and raucous pits, I was smitten with a numbing case of hero worship. Heyward walked him in. A smile crinkled his leathery face, a guileless wreath I rarely saw from people nearest me. Heyward brought him to where Wylie and One-Eye were standing next to a pair of cars, *Thunder Too* for Wylie and the other, and made the introductions. The afternoon was warm, not hot. Puffery clouds scampered through the crisp blue sky.

Nice car, said Rex to Wylie.

Wylie grumbled the acknowledgment.

This other one's yours, said Heyward. One-Eye, here, built it for you.

Rex looked it over carefully, like it wasn't a red-clay hot rod but the finest racing machine in the world. He checked over everything. Satisfied, he sat down in the driver's seat and strapped himself tight with the lap belt.

Seat okay? One-Eye asked.

Pretty close.

In height, Rex Harding might have been a horse jockey, but from years of racing Indy cars, his arms could wrestle bears.

Move it up a notch and it'll be about perfect, then, he said.

He turned to me, standing by, and winked. If I hadn't recently whizzed, I would have then.

Rex Harding next did something I'd never seen a race-car driver do whom I had ever known. He went to Heyward's tiny office, a shack down by the first turn, and when he came back . . . My God, he wore a real plastic crash helmet, not the leather things with narrow brims that Wylie and Spencer favored. Across the right breast of his driving uniform, all white and stiff with fireproofing solvent, was a single word, *Rex*, sewn in script. He wore driving gloves and he wore a pair of soft-leather shoes, tiny and floppy and colored a brilliant red and black. I could hear the silent snickers up and down the pits: Rex Harding, the greatest, toughest race-car driver in the country, done up like some fancy European playboy. Hoo-ha.

Wylie wore what he always raced in: a white T-shirt, khaki pants, and a pair of lace-up shoes that looked as though they'd been to war and back. In fact, they had. His lucky boots, Wylie called them.

My face flushed with embarrassment for Wylie. He looked like a sharecropper in the company of a city-slick banker. I looked at Wylie. His eyes blazed with hate.

It could have been a dicey day, but Rex showed from the start that he was a real race-car driver. He took the car out for a practice lap or two and immediately set to asking One-Eye, and Wylie, all sorts of questions about the car, the track, the other drivers. He wasn't condescending, not a whit, and after a while I could see Wylie coming back to himself.

After that, everybody got down to business. A racing afternoon it was, of the sort the Four Corners Speedway would see a hundred times in the years to come. Rex Harding qualified fourth and finished fourth. Spencer was third, Wylie second. Somebody I don't remember won the race, and that was almost that. Rex and Spencer got into each other a couple of times, but it was clear to all that Rex wasn't going to take any serious chances, not on vacation in a strange car and with five hundred dollars in his pocket just for showing up.

When the race was over, the fans swarmed down out of the grandstand and headed for the pits. More precisely, they headed for Rex Harding. They hung back, staring at him like he was a god, or something, which in fact is what I knew him well to be.

Suddenly, like she'd been spat out of the crowd, like a watermelon seed, Annalise marched up to Rex with a pencil and a piece of yellow school paper in her hand.

Mr. Harding, can I have your autograph? she asked.

You sure can, young lady, he said. What's your name?

Annalise. A-N-N-A-L-I-S-E. That's my daddy over there. He made up your car.

And did a mighty fine job, Rex said, scribbling his signature.

Wynn was next, my tomato-freckled friend. I wanted to melt into a crack and disappear.

105

That's my daddy that you run against, Wynn said, pointing to Spencer. He done beat you.

He's a good race-car driver, Rex laughed. Maybe I should ask him up to Indy so I can get back at him.

He'd beat you up there, too, Rex, Wynn said, all full of himself.

Now, Wynn, said Spencer. That's not being very polite to Mr. Harding.

You can call me Rex. And who's that little fellow standing next to you, Wynn?

Shit a brick, he was pointing at me. I edged to the front of the circle, and summoning courage from great depths, I, too, asked for my hero's autograph.

What's *your* name? he asked me, his pencil poised.

Andrew, I squeaked.

Andy?

No. Andrew.

I took the magic piece of paper and stood frozen at the spot. I could not command my legs to walk.

Tell you what, Andrew, let's you and me go for a ride.

Before I could protest or otherwise demur, Rex Harding picked me up with one arm and easily sat me inside his race car. It was a place I'd never been. Before Rex could say a word, Annalise and Wynn clambered in the back.

Y'all grab your best hold.

Rex turned the ignition and we grumbled out of the pits. We made two laps, he and I—I would not acknowledge the other passengers—slowly and safely, the rear end of the car breaking loose just enough to give me a little thrill. When the tour ended, there were now three serious cases of hero worship at the Four Corners Speedway. Wynn, Annalise, and I could just as well have been struck dumb.

That started a parade. A line formed, of sorts, and for the next half hour, Rex Harding, the greatest race-car driver in the country, took all who wanted on a tour of the Four Corners Speedway. Miss Ma, even, was persuaded, and Miss Dee, and even Uncle Julian hopped in for a ride—Uncle Julian, the quietest, sneakiest transporter in Stokes County.

Steak and tamales was the post-race meal, even for us kids, who maintained churchly silence. Talk was racing talk and Indianapolis pageantry.

At last, the day wore down.

That was a fine thing you did for the kids and everybody, One-Eye said to Rex by way of parting.

I enjoyed myself, he said. I enjoyed myself all day, as a matter of fact. Wylie, you got kids?

Silence.

Andrew here's my boy, he finally said.

Sure is a quiet one.

Yes, he's that. He worships you enough. I can't get him to come near my car. Maybe I'll have to send him to Indianapolis when he grows up. He doesn't like mine worth a shit.

The sprinkle of laughter that followed could not drown the truth.

Two months later, in midst of raw November, One-Eye brought the paper and showed the picture of the accident to Wylie.

Wylie looked.

So he done went and killed himself, is all he said, nothing more.

Who, Wylie? I asked. Who done killed himself?

That fellow back here in September. That Rex Harding fellow. That's who

One-Eye read the story. Rex had been in California

107

for the last race of his season, and in practice another driver was having trouble. Nothing serious—the car wouldn't go fast—and the other driver asked Rex to take the car and find some speed. Before Rex ever went on the race track, he checked over all parts of the car, his and anybody else's. Only this time he didn't. He just hopped in and drove away. He couldn't have known that the mechanics for the other car hadn't tightened the wing nut on the right-rear wheel. It worked loose, and Rex had maybe three seconds to know what was going to happen before it happened. The wheel came off as he entered a turn and the car must have flipped six or seven times. The picture showed the car, an open-cockpit Indy racer, sort of standing on its nose, with Rex, his arms askew, trying to fly out of it. He would have, maybe, if he hadn't cinched his seat belt. The last time down the car landed on its back, with Rex only half inside the cockpit. He never got hurt at the race track except the time he died there.

My heart split in two and I cried the biggest tears I had ever cried—none since as large—and nothing said by Wylie or Miss Ma, or even One-Eye, could make a difference.

Wylie finally got enough.

Stop that, boy, he said. Stop that carrying on. You'd think it was your own daddy got hurt and not a stranger.

I looked past Wylie like he wasn't there.

I wish he was my daddy, I said, even if he's dead.

Wylie coiled, his cobalt eyes a fury. He took a backhand swing and slapped me hard across my salt-stained cheek. He didn't hold back.

CHAPTER
12

The years rolled by. I made my passages in what had come to be my way, acquired a singular, introspective viewpoint of my town and kinfolks, friends. No passage, though, however final, worked to ease the passing of my Indy hero or Wylie's slap across my cheek. The memory of those doubly fatal blows were etched in silvery fire, never to recede.

Racing changed, make no mistake. The bullring circuit for the one-time whiskey cars grew in leaping bounds, with Wylie and Spencer, hot-dog heroes of contrasting moods and racing styles, in the middle thick of it. Gone for days and sometimes weeks, they were, returning home with stockpiled tales of savage comicry to regale the tables at Miss Dee's. Coincident with this, another Circuit came in being, where the latest cars from Motor City strutted sleek and low-slung before adoring throngs of tens of thousands and created for their knightly chauffeurs instant fame and glory, and, with a lucky break or two, grand golden riches,

too. Many from the bullring tour made fair transition—
Clyde Warden and Dink MacIntosh were best examples
of those who sought this golden ring with grand success;
many others tried and failed. Wylie Mavis and Spencer
Tatum never tried.

Too old, said Wylie. The way things are setting up
in racing, one of three things can happen. You can be
the big fish in the big pond, like Clyde and Dink. Or you
can be the small fish in the big pond. Or you can be the
big fish in the small pond.

Or, said One-Eye to be contrary, you can wind up
the small fish in the small pond, which a bunch of fellows
have.

Never crossed my mind, said Wylie. From the first
day, that never crossed my mind.

In my heart of hearts, said Spencer, a part of me
wants to be a big fish in the big pond, or at least test the
waters. I'd be lying to say different. But I know my limits
of what I can and cannot do. And besides that, racing's
racing. Once you get behind the wheel of a good race car
on a day when everything works just right, it doesn't make
a whole lot of difference if you're at Indianapolis, or running in a Circuit race somewhere in front of thirty thousand
people in a fancy new *Dee*-troit car, or running on the red
clay trying to figure a way. It just doesn't make a difference once you're out there running fenders and fenders,
doing the best you know. It just doesn't.

Yessir, chimed One-Eye, the money and the glory and
kissing all those doll-babies who give you the trophies and
all, that's nice, but that's not what plays in your mind when
the flag dips. Or, if it does, you'll just as likely go on a
squirrelly sail out of the race track.

They were so different, Wylie and Spencer. From my

watching, my impression was that Spencer didn't count the wins and losses, rather that—leastaways for him—the race-track ding-dong derring-do was so much icing on a cake. He kept no cabinet of trophies, save what Wynn and Mary scavenged from his shop where they'd been sent to discard, and when the conversation turned to racing triumphs, he demurred and twisted talk to how the cars were built and raced, and not his winning.

Tinkering Spencer. His race cars were his prizes. He spent hours over hours in his little cluttered shop behind his house, contriving ways to get a touch more corner handling, a straightaway flick of speed. His pensive wheels churned in both midday light and darkened dreams. Often he'd wake up beyond the midnight hour, quietly sneak from Mary's side, and tiptoe down the stairs and bolt out to the shop with the idea that had stunned him wide awake. There he'd fix a brimstone pot of coffee and tinker to the light. More than twice, tolerant Mary found her dreamy husband dead asleep on a fold-out cot he kept there for such purposes, covered from the sidereal chill by an oily blanket that had been lying there forever.

One-Eye often told the story.

Late one night—the time was two or three—One-Eye for unremembered reasons drove past Spencer's shop and saw a light and stopped, figuring for a cup of coffee at the least. There sat Spencer, cross-legged, back to door, staring at his car of the moment, polished as was always true to highest sheen. A single barren bulb cast a flickering dull light to the darkened corners.

Spencer heard the door but didn't move.

You know, One-Eye, he finally said to break the pause, I work and work on these race cars. I'm intimate with them, know exactly how they work and where they're strong and weak. I give reward for good performance, and even for a bad, and when they're hurt I fix them up. And I've only got one question.

What's that, Spencer?

Why won't they talk to me?

Spencer laughed and One-Eye laughed, but none too loudly. For One-Eye, too, was sympathetic with Spencer's plea. He understood the special relationship between a mechanic and his racing car, and how it differed from the one between the car and driver.

To a driver, One-Eye said, a race car is just a means. But to a mechanic, the car's an end in itself. When that green flag drops, the race car's as good as it's going to get, and frankly, I'm always a little sad whenever I turn one of those babies over to a driver. He can't make it better, but he sure can bloody its nose. The driver tries to get more from a car than the car has to give. They're all at odds; the mechanic and his car never are. They may fight and squabble now and then, but there's a lasting bond that drivers cannot understand.

Try that out on Wylie, I thought, for a change of pace. No, Wylie was a different sort. Mean and glumly troubled, he raced to win and only that. The cars he drove were of no more consequence than a piece of processed cheese.

On the race track, their polarity was similar. Spencer won the races he should have won, and didn't win the races he should have lost. He didn't push, didn't prod, drove smoothly flag to flag. He calculated, mind you, sought to find a way, but if he couldn't, no matter then, he'd bring his car home safely and run again next day.

Wylie scaled the heights and found the hidden valleys. Wylie wasn't erratic so much as he was spectacular. And brutal. He'd be two laps down with ten to go—no chance to win and getting blasted everywhere—and when the leaders tickled his tail to lap him once again, Wylie'd stay there hunkered down in the middle of the racing groove and dare the bastards by. Such tenacity was cause for admiration now and then, so I suppose, but it wasn't the stuff of lasting friendships. Wylie was not a favorite on the bullring tour.

Once I tried to break the barriers of our distraught alienation. I praised him on a Wylie-ferocious ride, one that brought him fifth to second in a race's waning laps.

If I'd known when the race began that I was going to be a second, Wylie said, I never would have taken up the flag.

Such polarity between the two. Such disparate different sorts. The fragile tolerance each carried for the other could not last. The wonder's that it held as firmly as it did.

Near the end of season 1956, the title points for the Four Corners Speedway's ten-race driving season were close. On a Sunday afternoon in mid-September was run the seventh of the ten, a flat-out dash of fifty laps. Wynn strapped in Spencer, No. 20; I and One-Eye buckled Wylie, No. 7. They punched their starter buttons; their cars and eighteen others roared to life.

The first third of the race, fifteen laps or so, was quiet. Wylie, starting from the second row, won a joust with Johnny Ashman, then punched Harry Baker to the rail and slid his way to first. Spencer ran the other way. Starting sixth, by ten laps' time he'd fallen back to tenth; by fifteen laps he'd motivated backward to a baker's-dozen thirteenth. Spencer yielded these positions easily. He ran high and low, but never did a thing to fight the others going by. He might have been out there alone.

I looked at Wynn to question what was what.

Goddamn, Daddy, he muttered, get something going.

Then Spencer stopped his backward march. For five laps just—I counted—Wylie kept his margin. I punched my stopwatch to confirm suspicions. With twenty down and thirty laps to go, Wylie's lead was twelve seconds flat. The next time by, 11.5; the next time after that, eleven flat. The fisherman was reeling in his fish, one half second to the lap.

Now was when Spencer's gentlemanly attitude paid dividends. Just as Spencer hadn't fought the other cars that once had passed him by, so now did they decline to argue Spencer's sudden charge. The others didn't yield the racing groove—Spencer had to pick the time and place to make his passes—but neither did they block the track once Spencer got them by. I watched the pretty sight with cool admiration, as did the crowd and other crews, once they had picked up on Spencer's doings. Nine seconds; seven; five; four.

The deal was simple enough. Wylie and One-Eye had set their *Thunder Too* in hope of running at the front from flag to flag; Wylie knew no other way. Spencer had tinkered his to find the quickest passage later on. One lap counted only, number fifty. To Spencer, the in-between was merely research and development.

Soon Spencer roosted on Wylie's tail, and here stepped out of character to cavort, at Wylie's expense. On the straights Spencer played a drum roll on Wylie's bumper, rat-a-tat-tat, nothing devious, but forceful enough to get his message firmly through. Off number two with eight laps left, Spencer feinted high, and when Wylie drifted high to block, Spencer cut beneath him and was gone. It would have been a competitive pass except there was no competition.

Wylie raged, lost ten car lengths off the bat, and started back as best he could. Wynn grinned back at me; I turned my head.

Wylie drove possessed, charged ten, fifteen, twenty feet deeper into the turns than he had any right to go. The closest he could get to Spencer was to nose his car beneath Spencer's left-rear quarterpanel, no more. He'd have to back off or risk a marbly slide. For two laps thusly, Wylie challenged, twice a lap. On the white-flag lap, the last, they entered one as before: Spencer high on a string; Wylie nosed in down low at the teeter-totter point.

Spencer turned into the turn and Wylie didn't. He T-boned Spencer at the pillar. Spencer, sliding to the right, put on the binders, but fractions later slammed the bandy rail and punched it through. Wylie, likewise, followed Spencer out, but not as cleanly. He clipped a guard-rail post and nearly ripped his engine from its mount.

So quickly had the stunning deed been done that stormy silence was the only quick response. The starter red-flagged the race, and I and others ran for the hole in the turn, not knowing what we'd see on the far side. The choices seemed to be two badly injured drivers or a whale of a fistfight. There was neither. Both sat in their cars, dazed and groggy. Wylie bled from a forehead cut, the only obvious injury.

What happened, Wylie? One-Eye asked, panting from his run.

Throttle stuck, said Wylie, the wildness gone.

Bullshit, you son of a bitch, said Wynn, a tethered bull. Stuck throttle, my ass. You tried to kill my daddy. You punched him out of there because he was whipping your butt.

Wylie looked at Wynn quizzically, drained of response, said nothing, reached to wipe the superficial blood from his brow. A quiet silence loomed as large as the gaping hole in Heyward Scrivens's guard rail, until there came a strange, distended voice.

If my old man wanted to kill your daddy, your chickenshit daddy would be dead.

The voice was mine. In cold fury I moved toward Wynn, slowly and precisely, measuring carefully for the distance left between us. It never occurred to me that, given the disparity in our adolescent bulk, I was about to be cold-cocked into the next century.

Dozier McCartle thought similarly. He interposed himself between us, face to face with me, and One-Eye bound up Wynn. The moment was comic, in a way: two surrogates being held apart while the men whose honor they sought to defend sat stunned in the background shadows.

That was the end of it, for me, but not for Wynn. A week he brooded, sulked; stayed far from Spencer and the little shop behind their house. But restless confusion, no surprise, won him over late one mid-week night. Sad and troubled, he walked into the shop.

Need help, dad? he asked.

Always do, said Spencer, staring at a crumpled left-front fender. Grab some gloves and hold this out a-ways so I can cut it off.

Wynn did, with muscle-bulging ease, and volunteered other aids, while dancing round the reason for his coming.

Why'd you let Wylie come after you? Wynn finally asked.

Wasn't a hell of a lot I could do, said Spencer, his back to Wynn. He didn't turn left. His throttle stuck.

116

Bull, daddy. The son of a bitch tried to run you over.

Some drivers are stupid, Wynn. Others are lousy. I haven't met one yet who's suicidal.

He went crazy on you.

Maybe. A little. But he wouldn't do a thing to me that would hurt him, too, now, would he? He got the worst. If he'd hit that rail post another foot toward center, the engine of his car would have snapped his backbone. You don't take chances like that, not even Wylie.

Wynn pressed on.

Everybody saw Wylie didn't turn, he said. Didn't try to turn. He didn't give a damn about himself. He tried to T-bone you into eternity. Why do you make his excuses?

I've raced that man long enough to know what he's capable of.

And afterward, said Wynn, reaching to the nugget. Afterward, you didn't go after him. You didn't call him.

There was no need. Wylie was hurt. What was done was done.

That's not good enough, Daddy. If I hadn't said something, nobody named a Tatum would have taken note.

I'm proud of you for standing up, make no mistake. But there was no need. Wylie knew what was going on and so did I. That's what matters.

Well, now. You tell *me* what went on. From where I stood, I guess I couldn't see it all as clear as you.

Wylie was frustrated, Spencer said, without a reference to Wynn's sarcasm. He wasn't handling worth a damn and I could go wherever on the track I wanted.

Damn, Spencer smiled. I was dialed in—ano Wylie got a little flustered.

And that gives him license?

Jesus, son, said Spencer, a vocal tightness creeping in,

if I had known he was going to crash me, deliberate or not, I would have made it a point to be somewhere else.

Where else? said unreconciled Wynn. In the pits? That would have been safe enough, wouldn't it? In the pits. Or maybe in the stands with Mom and Miss Ma and Melvina.

Wynn was oblivious to the fine line he'd just crossed.

What do you mean? asked Spencer.

Wynn backed down, but little.

Daddy, you are the prettiest race-car driver I have ever seen. When that car's set right, you can drive it with one finger and I'm so proud I can't stand it. But you back off. If you weren't my daddy, I'd say you were a coward. I know you're not—you're not, are you? But when somebody takes a thing away from you, you don't fight to gain it back. Andrew was pissed at me just for calling Wylie names. And you're sitting there scratching your head.

First off, said mildly jut-jawed Spencer, how am I supposed to do anything when my car's sitting fifty feet outside the race track and they've done red-flagged the race? Second off, do you know me so little to think that my winning the race *or* beating Wylie Mavis, in any way, is important to me? I know what people are going to remember about that race. They're going to remember the wreck, and the words that went between you and Andrew. But you know what I'm going to remember?

What's that, daddy?

I'm going to remember that I thought a problem through long and hard, and that on that afternoon I got a maximum performance out of me and out of that car. Looking through my mirror at Wylie, frantic and akimbo, was *so* much fun. There wasn't a way he was going to get past me clean if we'd raced another two hundred laps. I didn't need a checkered flag to tell me that. And I don't need to punch out Wylie to remind me.

His throttle didn't stick, said Wynn again, subdued. He didn't just try to push you out of the way. We all saw it—except you. You ignored it. And now you protect a man who's tried to kill you. Anyplace else than here and Wylie'd be hanging from a tree.

Wylie's a difficult man, said Spencer. He's been through a lot. He deserves some of your sympathy.

I'm gonna have to go after him, said Wynn, declining Spencer's argument.

How's that, son?

He can't do such a thing and not be accused.

He stands accused, Wynn. Trust me. He stands accused.

By who, Daddy? You and he'll go off racing again and it'll be just like old times. You'll slam and bang—rather, he'll slam and bang and you'll back off and buy the beers after.

You don't mean what you say.

I don't mean all of it, but enough.

Wynn was close to bursting, his tomato face colored to a beet.

Don't do anything foolish, Spencer said. Or careless.

I'll do what I've got to do.

Be careful.

. . .

So such a dialogue reached my ears. And so the moment bloodhound Wynn took up his racing, though he would not begin in earnest for four more years. My goad, of similar dimensions, was six years down the way. But still its germ—I later thought—was well related to the one that fevered friend and rival, Wynn.

CHAPTER 13

Some races, no explaining, take on lives of their own. By the upbeat tingle in the air, you know that something special looms. One such race was Heyward's first of 1957, a special invitational for all cars no matter what their age or engine size, a grab-bag confab of rich and famous Circuit cars, should any dare appear, mixed in with iron stallions of the local heroes—the rules be damned and grab your tightest hold.

The winter past was short but glum. Gray and misty clouds poured over the distant mountains at the changing of the season and parked atop Four Corners for eight weeks even, nothing more or less, and forced the souls beneath to sullen contemplation. Not a friendly time, all this, but still it served a purpose. Talk, not action, was the hallmark of the winter's wait. Wynn and I resumed a civil discourse, though its nature would never have the free and casual bounce of once before. But, when Heyward asked Miss Dee for sugar tea in confirmation of the winter's passing, the scene began to form for what would be the high-point bullring race of all our lives.

The race was named the Dogwood 100. Heyward's imagination would not allow a designation fancier. The date, postponed a week by rain, was April 21 of 1957—Easter Sunday, no need to check the calendar. As the magic afternoon drew near, so did amorphous anticipation build and billow, flamed by winds of springtime's soft renewal. Spencer burned the midnight hours for days on end; One-Eye, and even Wylie, did the same, tuning fine the myriad parts of *Thunder Too*, by now the fifth of Wylie's cars to bear that name. Though I had long since overpaid my joy-ride debt to Wylie, I, too, did my share, drawn in to such pursuits against my will and younger instincts.

The weather heated up, beyond all charted expectations. Easter morning broke in soft and brilliant light. The day would not be merely warm but dog days' summer hot, fanned by a bristling southern wind that everywhere raised dust, including at the race track. The undue heat was joined by untoward drought. The creeks still flowed a lively torrent from the distant mountains' snow-melt, but that was all the water to be had. With hellacious effort, Heyward worked a losing battle to shape his winter-dormant bullring for the fray.

Easter services at Will Rollins's whitewashed one-room Baptist worship hall were done at sunrise for the true devout, and at ten o'clock for guilt-struck once-a-years, where all assorted Mavises stood for counting. Preacher Will chose this day to doubly rail against his favorite sins of demon rum and thunder race cars, though canny Heyward, not the fool, had asked the preacher to give the pre-race invocation, and the preacher, closer to a fool by far, and sensing a tenfold increase in his congregation, had accepted.

And so we gathered in the stultifying heat, the men and boys in mothballed suits and ties never seen save wedding day and funeral, while the women and the girls broke out white and lily-flowered, white-gloved and ribbon-hatted. Midway through the service—this, around eleven, as perspiration poured from glistening foreheads— I saw Heyward, not one to play the hypocrite no matter what his other inclinations, sneak into the back of the church and sidle up to One-Eye.

They're coming, he whispered.

One-Eye passed the word to Spencer, who tossed it on to Wynn, who moved across the center aisle and told Julian and Melvina, who told Miss Ma, who told Wylie, whose eyes ignited as he told me.

Though Heyward thought they might appear, he'd feared to say too loudly until he could confirm. But he had witnessed for himself, just now, the cars of Clyde Warden and Dink MacIntosh being towed past Colonel Stokes to the race track. Well, after that, you might have thought he'd seen a UFO instead. The sedate buzz that riffled through the congregation reached such proportion that poor Will, whose flockly hold was less than absolute in best of circumstance, sent the nervous choirmaster, Harold Peabody, loping to the back to find its cause. Still, the service moved along at Will's tedious pace, did not appear to head for early denouement. At twenty minutes to noon, Will continued to ramble on, though not oblivious to the general stir. At ten of noon, those rearward in the gathering slyly took their leave. By twelve chimes on the nose, the restlessness ascended to a shuffling, muffled roar, and Will, like any comprehending general who knows the battle's lost, sounded quick and orderly retreat.

And the Lord keep you and be with you always, he said. The closing hymn. One verse only.

Harold played the final Resurrection dirge at double speed. When done, the congregation broke. Clyde Warden and Dink MacIntosh were coming to town.

There's none to tell how good Clyde Warden and Dink MacIntosh might have been. They were fine race-car drivers as it was, Circuit stars the equal in our parts of Rex Harding in his. But the count of races they should have won, in opposition to those they actually did, was truly staggering. They raced Fords and Chryslers, Chevrolets and Dorsens, bouncing on a rubber band from one car to another in proportion to the patience of their many bosses—Jean-Pierre Andriotti, naming one.

Why did you fire them? reporters asked Jean-Pierre.

Because they fucked up and hit the fucking wall, was Jean-Pierre's less than casual reply.

Why did you hire them back? the same reporters sought to query later, maybe weeks or months.

Because they were leading the fucking race when they hit the fucking wall.

Jean-Pierre called them his race-track Laurel and Hardy. He was referring to how they slam-bam banged each other around the various Circuit stops. In appearance, unlike their driving, they were polar opposites. Clyde was the skinny one. He didn't look strong enough to punch out a shoe box, and, in fact, he was disinclined to brawling. But if provoked by serious intent or pixie funning, either, he could lay you out as quickly as another. Dink was different. He had the boxcar dimensions of a pro football middle guard, and little of his ample bulk was sloppy weight. Off the track, he never fought: didn't have to. On the track, he had the disposition of a gypsy comic, and it was usually he who goaded Clyde into the demolition altercations of the sort that so distracted Jean-Pierre.

Heyward Scrivens had invited them to satisfy his curiosity, nothing else, and wasn't really banking for reply. Indeed, there hadn't been one until their two alabaster Dorsens, each towed behind an alabaster pickup truck, made appearance to the Colonel. One of the mechanics said Clyde and Dink were still in Terminus, but shortly would fly in.

How shortly? asked Heyward.

What time's the race? asked one mechanic.

Practice at one, qualifying at two, the flag at three.

They'll be here by the flag, the mechanic said languidly.

Hoo-boy, said Heyward, rolling his sunglassed eyes.

The evidence was soon at hand that whatever had given this race a special aura within Four Corners had done its work in other parts as well. There was just the one road to the track from town—Highway 77—and Dozier one-wayed it northbound as soon as church let go. Well, by one o'clock, the time of practice start, I stood on tippy-toes atop a flatbed truck inside the infield and looked to meet the gaze of Colonel Stokes, and saw not two but four lanes of traffic pouring toward the track. Heyward and Dozier weren't ready for this. One ticket seller and another for the taking awaited the throng, an operation that was quickly over-matched.

Poor Heyward. Poor Dozier. They were out there by the gate themselves, trying as best they could to park the cars and, more important, collect the fiver—the normal fare was two—that Heyward in his knowing greediness had picked to charge that day. They were frantic, running up and down the twice-doubled line of cars, stuffing greenbacks by the wad into their pants and shirts and hats, whatever there was handy. I roared to see such avarice rewarded, and turned attention back to race-track doings.

Lord, was it dusty. I wished Heyward would have spent less time collecting money and more to dampen down the red-clay mist. Once practice started, the water truck did moisten down the track every fifteen minutes. A futile gesture, for the blasty breezes dried the track as quickly and as thoroughly as Heyward's meager crew could wet it. I looked across the track into the stands, and giggled once again. All the girls and women still retained their churchly Easter finery, and right before my eyes it turned a copper brown of various shade and hue. Such were the dimensions of the building cloud of dust that I, for certain, knew that once the race got under way, those fans farthest from the level of the track would not be seeing this event so much as listening to it.

Qualifying started on the nose at two and in the dust. Thirty cars each took a trial for the twenty starting places; the ten that didn't make the Dogwood field would run a soothing consolation dash.

Among those that didn't qualify were Clyde's and Dink's. The big-fish heroes were not there, a fact of mixed emotions to nearly all. Wylie and Spencer, though keeping silent, wanted desperately to fly their flags against these legendary Circuit heroes. Once or twice a year is all the chance they got to show what might have been. Heyward's thoughts were elsewhere.

If I tell this crowd here they're not showing, he lamented, we'll have an Easter riot on our hands for sure.

You can't hold off forever, said Wylie.

Besides, said One-Eye, qualifying's closed. What's fair for us is fair for them, no matter who they are.

Heyward waited, pulled delays as long as he could, then glumly announced, but only to the crews and drivers in the pits, that qualifying was closed.

Line up the cars for the consolation, he said, perspiring bullets.

At the instant of Heyward's flop sweat, we heard a dim and distant buzz from the south, then two, a brace of nagging houseflies. At the next instant we in the pits dived for cover as two single-engine planes swooped in low over the three-four turn and buzzed the race track to within ten feet of the ground. The pilots waggled their wings and waved.

They're here, said the languid Dorsen mechanic, not bothering to look up.

The nonplussed starter gathered his wits and threw the flag to get the consolation under way. Clyde and Dink tight-circled aimlessly until the ten-lap race was over, then landed side by side on a grassy knoll behind the back straight. They chockblocked their planes, and to the grandstand's hearty roar walked across the track to where Heyward stood surrounded by the cluster of Dogwood drivers.

Heyward circled his wagons as best he could, his problem doubly magnified. Bad enough to say that Clyde and Dink wouldn't race because they hadn't shown, worse yet to say they couldn't race when they were there for all to see.

Glad you made it, he said in greeting, but qualifying's closed. I can't let you run without a time trial like the others had to make.

Aaw, Heyward, said Clyde, his lanky grin spread billboard wide, don't let the money be a hindrance.

We don't want the purse, said Dink. The racing's what we came for. Let us line up at the rear and run for free. We'll not take money that we haven't truly earned.

There was a pause while Heyward pleaded their case to Wylie, Spencer, and the others. The settlement was quick.

Sounds fair, said Wylie.

Thus was the lineup set. Twenty whiskey hot-rod cars lined up in equal rows of two; behind them in row eleven, Clyde and Dink, unqualified and unconcerned. The green flag fell on the halcyon afternoon and started off one hell of a damn good race.

Clyde and Dink came ripping through the pack, as was expected. The first half of the field was easy pickings. By twenty laps the Circuit stars rode tenth and twelfth. But then the broil started. The front-runners, more accustomed to the wayward markings of the whorish half-mile ring, were not so easily subdued. By fifty laps, the halfway count, Wylie was third, Spencer fifth, Dink sixth, and Clyde eighth—with Wylie nearly one lap to the good of Clyde and perched grimly on his tail.

There matters stood for ten laps, more, no change, as a dust cloud from the roaring pack clogged sweating pores and teared the eyes.

On sixty-one, Dink hooked Spencer, spun him out. I couldn't figure why. Probably he was testing whether Spencer had the same sense of humor belonging to his side-kick, Clyde. Spencer, his car undamaged by the minor ding-dong, more or less kept going, gave no hint of seeking retribution. Wylie, though, saw matters through a different prism. Had the transgressor been any but one of the Circuit heroes, and the victim anyone but Spencer, he no doubt would have let the matter pass. But Wylie's often cluttered sense of fairness was offended. I knew his lack of love for Spencer was profound, but this was down to cases: them or us.

Wylie took out after Dink, for all to see. He blew by Clyde, then passed Spencer, and in a furious lap or two he got to Dink and simply pushed him in the fence. Dink's radiator geysered steam. He limped back to the pits and parked.

Now was Clyde's turn to take up the fallen banner of a buddy. He caught up Wylie, tried every trick in his driver's book to crash him, but Wylie, on a sacred drive, found deep tenacity and would not let this interloper do him in. What a grand engagement, for Wylie's spirit had touched a prideful nerve in Clyde, no slouch, all knew, at such debates.

Clyde caught Wylie time and time again, but could not pass. Both were lapped by other cars. No matter. Their hoary duel had gained dimension far beyond the win or lose. At one point—what the lap was, none could tell—Clyde chopped the first turn low and hard, more or less creating his own race track, and aimed to T-bone Wylie, much as Wylie had done Spencer months before. A small gasp escaped the standing, roaring crowd as the Circuit hero's goal came clear. But at the last split second before the hit, Wylie absolutely stood on his brakes. Clyde, not so quick, shot past his bow and bammed the rail. Hard.

That ended matters on the track, but only there. The words began in the pits, even before the two proud and furious gladiators had escaped their cars, and this time no foolish intercession would have a calm effect. By the time the checkers flew—who got the trophy, I don't know—they were brawling like a pair of rutting moose. Clyde never lost his sense of humor, totally; Wylie never had one there to lose. While the insults stayed one-sided, the fight was even up, even as it grew.

The first to join, of all surprises, was Annalise. She jumped the grandstands, ran across the track as best she could, still fitted up in Easter wear, once white, now dusty brown, a sight. She climbed all over poor Clyde's back, no easy task, and pulled his hair and damn near clawed his eyes out. That was the signal. I picked up a screwdriver, thought better of my weapon choice, and entered the fray on Wylie's side, carried by confused emotions I never stopped to sort. Then Wynn popped in. He would have had a cause whichever side he picked, chose neither, stayed only long enough to pull away a rather startled Annalise. Julian, from a corner of my eye, shrugged a shoulder in a brother's resignation and waded in when Wynn and Annalise had waded out, and threw a trio of less than fatal punches. Dink, the onetime instigator of this strange confabulation, started over, was deterred by One-Eye on the one arm and Spencer on the other. They backed away, their five eyes twinkling, soon were split-side laughing at the sight of Clyde Warden, Circuit superstar, more or less engaged with all the virile members of the Mavis clan.

Miss Ma was late arriving, but no less decisive for her tardiness. She grabbed a tire iron, nothing less, and, before a warning could be sounded, struck Clyde three fiercely matriarchal times across his right kneecap. Clyde took notice, as well he might, and declined a further challenge.

I can't take on the whole Mavis family by myself, he said, his smile as undiminished as before.

Well, damn if you weren't doing a pretty good job of it, shouted Dink for all to hear.

Thanks for your help, darling, Clyde said.

That broke the air. The battle ceased. The onetime foes shook hands, assayed the minor damages, and offered apologies profuse and reasonably sincere.

The dust cloud sank, exhausted. As if they'd been through this a hundred times before, the two grand Circuit warriors bid adieu and staggered off across the track, and soon, with farewell waggles of their wings, were off.

CHAPTER 14

. . . Was I knocked out by my ride-the-rail? I don't know; don't much care. By some saucy physic miracle my car declines to totter to the parking lot below, but teeters to the race track, though my accident, I fear, has just begun.

Make no mistake, I am afraid. My car clambers down with yet another grating roar, and I am afraid. I fear for the ruined car, whose gemlike brilliance so enthralled me and filled my soaring heart with pride and joy upon first viewing last night on the cobbled square beneath the Colonel's gaze. The car can be replaced, I know, at a cost to only lightly lessen the Dorsen money bucket. But in my brief conjugality with it I've felt a bond stronger than I, no doubt, had any right to feel. Not sexual, lusting silliness, no. But this car, and only it, was there to do my bidding, take me places of my dreams, and for me win a ransom of strong and good performances. With every banshee sound and bit of bending, twisting, broken metal, the car is tearing from my grasp, never mine to drive again. I see again, in my mind's eye, my name in tiny letters on its brilliant white door. That's what I'll remember of her, no matter how this all turns out. And make no second mistake, I fear for myself. Now I've gathered time to recollect my thoughts, though groggy and pain-shocked from the collision. If this were over now, I'd tremble at its recent memory. Maybe on the morn I'd laugh and regale clutching, clinging listeners with the story of my surviving such a wham-bang bash, but I know that in addition to the other tolls I'll pay, my race-car driver's psyche is being altered by this little la-di-da in a most prominent way. The memory of the humpy-bump, I know, I'll be able to recall as brightly as my name beneath the window of my door, and of my action when next I round that grizzly turn with, as one example, Wynn close up in front of me, what will I do? I'll yield just a tick of time, is what, and wait another lap, or two, or three to make my pass. My trophy case has been diminished by this joyless, brutal ride. I am staring at eternity from a distance much foreshortened, and I don't care lots for what I see. It's a matter of perspective, and I'd rather keep an arm's length while I can.

But this fear has also truly calmed me. I observe with strange disinterestedness that the focus of my concentration is even narrower than it was mere seconds ago. Yes, I am afraid at several places, but I sense with grim-glum satisfaction that I am reacting well, even as I realize that it's grace allowing me to react at all.

Whose fault, all this? The car's, or mine, or bloodhound Wynn's? No time for such extraneousness. No time.

The engine lives! A shrilly roaring fills the entrails of my wounded steed. I still have racing power, fully, and thus a choice to make: to in this instant punch the kill switch, a bright-red glowing button at the center of the steering column, and lose the largest measure of control, or work the throttle with an aching foot and try to loop my savaged car and scrub the greatest portion of my fatal speed. The relentless grating continues undiminished; the car fills up with acid smoke—rubber, oil, gas, I cannot tell—watering my already blurry eyes.

I cadge a fuzzy glance on down the track and see that Wynn himself is in a dusty, tire-smoking slide, but in control and safely off the wall. Did I clip him? Who's to say? Or did he swivel wrongly as a devious result of my dogged, fiery pursuit? A fair revenge, if so, though not intended. Dear Wynn, my destiny, what have our little games of childhood brought on? A final destination?

I am aimed for the apex of the dogleg, the place, though under different circumstance, I'd wished to be. Between the race track, bowed out here along the main straight, and the pit road there's a grassy interlude; farther beyond, another bandy ribbon of steel just this side of the pit road itself. If my speed's diminished any, I cannot tell. The cockeyed angle of my travel puts all in new perspective. The whiny engine races, and I shamble on.

I choose. I twist the steering wheel hard left and punch the throttle, hoping for a slide. There's no response from either place. The gas pedal is slack and unresponsive; the steering wheel spins free. Again, I try this desperate maneuver, and still again, but all is shattered underneath. Throttle cables are snapped and lifeless; steering arms are broken, useless. With mild curiosity I search for the brakes, but these I cannot even find.

Now the left front of my car collapses, settles in, and I detect potential for salvation. The car twists left slightly, begins a slide. There's hope.

But no. Just as I begin this twist, I leave the track and hit the smooth and soothing grass. Abruptly the awful grating sounds diminish to a vicious hiss. My bilious stomach sinks, one horror now replaced by yet another. No longer does my car grapple with the asphalt, a war, however unequal, that at least has served to down my speed a smidgen; instead, it skates on grass with undiminished speed. Indeed, the loosened shackles give me a sense of increasing speed. I am totally denied control. I am in a plane plummeting from the sky in deathly spiral, a landlocked rocket without guidance.

Yet my destination is clear. The inner guard rail looms close-hauled near.

What do I do? What can I do?

How bad?

With slow, deliberate calmness born of panic desperation, I search for support. Still slung low in my contoured driver's seat, wedged against my crotch strap, I struggle to retrieve a sit position—all this with mild success. I place my legs on portions of the roll cage, left and right, which, up to now at least, is near intact. I grasp the steering wheel with both hands, denying the knife-blade pain in my right thumb, and feel the soft stickiness of the tape ooze between my fingers. I close my eyes. I lay my head atop the steering column, though I do not pray the Lord my soul . . . That possibility I will not yet admit.

I wait, hearing only the serpentine hiss as I slide to the rail.

The windshield shatters on this second impact. Tinkling shards of glass tingle my hands and face. The car lifts from the rear and starts a rightward roll.

I've lost my grip. My shoulder harness snaps; my seat belt breaks. I am free of all restraints, a rag dog flying loose within the confines of the roll cage, held in by nothing more than laws of nature and the brutal mercy of a mindless God.

In this tumbling turbulence I note—how strange a focus—that the black box, too, is free and flies: Jean-Pierre's black box, set there in part to measure my response to race-track things. What I wouldn't give to see the feedback from its readout now.

My mind is clear. My mind is all too clear . . .

CHAPTER
15

Full of surprises, full of himself, Wylie gave me the car for my eighteenth birthday.

It's yours, he said. You earned it.

Maybe so, come to think. It was the Ford that Wynn and I had christened on our ding-dong joyride passage long ago. I'd tweaked and putzed it long beyond repayment, and had, with One-Eye's kind solicitations, found some speed-shop tricks past meager showroom specs. Put back together once and finally, that little baby would flat-out *run*. The gift was just in time; improved my infirm adolescent popularity by leaps and bounds, especially—mix the blessing—with a certain Annalise.

Up to then she'd drifted in my life and out, a sullen migrant butterfly, a chum, a pal, no more, farmed out to our house or the Tatums', often, when One-Eye with the drivers hit the bullring circuit road.

I indulged her, One-Eye said. She was mine and all I had. I tried to raise her in a way of Mae's approving. Did I?

I don't know. She was beautiful at the start, got more so with the years, and what God declined to give her she contrived to make herself. She let her hair grow to her waist —could I object?—and every morn and night, I set my watch, she'd brush one hundred strokes, no more, no less. Nail polish, rouge, and makeup kits and creams of all dimensions—things of which I knew so little—were hers at a command. She'd sit before a mirror—the kind with lights that movie stars so favored—and dwell for hours in her world of make-believe. Yet sad she was, so very sad, and nothing of my father's love could offer solace for her dry-eyed tears. Uncomprehending, helpless, I watched her grow.

Annalise brought tickles to my groin, and others', too, if school and street-talk whispers had their merit. For me, the moment when she passed from gangly, long-haired buddy-chum to tawny Annalise—I need no photographic consort to jog the memory of this one sweet and bitter instant—was the high-point Easter brawl of that springtime past when she flailed about Clyde Warden's lanky, startled self. From the corner of my eye I saw Wynn grasp her tiny waist and pull her from the fray, an alabaster goddess dusted angry brown. Such a sudden pang of jealousy I felt as Wynn close-held her arched and twisting body; such envy and regret.

I couldn't say whether Annalise was drawn to me or to my car, such was the close conjunction. But drawn to us she was. Though she by then was one year passed from high school, she more than once contrived to be alone beside my car door, needing a desperate ride home or else-where—anywhere. Well, then, how could I refuse?

Or at the shop. I still had not yet found the goad to drive a race car, but by then the working on them filled the total of my free-time hours. One-Eye's mill shop—for there, despite the Heyward chill, was where Wylie's cars were treated—was surely One-Eye's domain still, but racing thrice and four times weekly, sometimes more at bullring season's height, cinched the hours and strapped the powers of the two-man operation. There was always one car ready for the track and another in the sick bay—true of all such operations, more so ours, when one recalled the nature of Wylie's angry drives. With certitude, the sick-bay car would always have a crumpled fender here and there, and in addition, One-Eye never shut his brain to improvising ways to make his tried-and-tested product even better. Between the two concerns, it was a chore just keeping up. Wylie didn't know exactly all that One-Eye did of engines and of chassis, but he had mastered how to relay information on the feeling of the race car foot by foot around the track, and with such certain knowledge One-Eye burned the moonlight hours in pursuit of greater speed and durability. I myself drew closer still to One-Eye's thinking. I had the knack. Given time and space in which to work, I found a way of staring almost any race-car problem into fair submission.

Often Annalise joined One-Eye at the shop, would sit and stare, would then announce she had good reason to skip on home and could I offer her the trip.

Please?

Well, how could I refuse?

And so it went with knockout tawny Annalise. She sat, always, in the snuggly center of the front seat, right where I couldn't help but notice her, right where a somebody looking by might confuse who was and wasn't driving. Perfume flowered the air. Arms brushed arms, and thighs touched thighs. Her red-singed golden hair brought my ears to stiff attention, and that's not all. I grappled to find the gearshift. Her face alone was ransom's price: cheekbone-high triangular, lush and pouty lips, round brown eyes that stared into distracted infinity. Always, at her house she waited for response to her fond and fondling invitation. Always, I declined, walked her quickly to the door.

Good night.

The door slammed, always.

But, though I was tempted, my gaze was aimed in other ways, in vicinity of Betsy Potter, another sort of girl altogether—so my thinking went—who, by way of squaring circles, offered me the same short shrift that I awarded Annalise.

Always, when I flustered back to the sanctity of *Thunder Too* and company, One-Eye asked the silent question with a smiling eyebrow raised. I know he would have blessed the match.

When One-Eye turned to home at completion of his work, Annalise was in a fury, always, locked behind her bedroom door, immersed in records and movie magazines.

Be patient, honey, would One-Eye say in fatherly confusion.

I don't have time to be patient, was tawny Anna's bitter, foul response. I don't have time.

One night . . . One night Annalise went to the shop, found Wylie waxing and polishing a quarterpanel he'd bent out, having found a wall somewhere.

Close the door, said Wylie.

With both hands he pushed a skin-soft chamois cloth hard up and down the glistening metal, not looking up.

Where's daddy? asked Annalise. I thought he and Andrew would be here.

Andrew's doing schoolwork, I suspect. One-Eye's run down to Terminus to pick up a couple of spindles. I reckon he'll be back within the hour. I crunched this baby pretty good. Brakes gave out. Sit down, if you'd like.

He motioned to a legless beat-up couch, rescued from the junk pile years before, for resting.

Annalise sat—made up, perfumed, dressed to kill as usual. Neither spoke. The thickening silence threatened to suffocate them both.

You and Andrew getting along? asked Wylie.

Not so you could notice, she replied. What does he say? Not that I much care.

Andrew's like me in some regards, said Wylie. Doesn't tell much of his goings-on.

With me, there's nothing much for him to say. I might as well be a tree, for all he cares.

He's a fool for that, said Wylie. But there's others. Wynn, for one. Looking at you, I can't see the problem.

Wynn's barely seventeen, a boy. How could I go out with such a young one? Even if I wanted?

Andrew's not a full year older than Wynn.

But he's different, more mature. He's halfway.

Between what and what? asked Wylie, turning now.

Oh, I don't know. Between Wynn and . . . between Wynn and you—or somebody like you.

Wylie paused, considered, let stuffy silence once again descend.

Want me to help you rub that thing down? asked Annalise.

Her quavering voice split the cloud of silence like a thunderclap. Wylie looked at her with fiery silver nuggets, his racing eyes. He didn't speak a word. He wiped his barnacled hands on the soft chamois cloth and walked across the chasm to the legless couch where Annalise lay, and there, with double-dactyl rhythm amid the dank and clutter of a dirt-track bullring speed shop, he took her. He didn't rape her, didn't seduce her—if Annalise resisted, it never made the record—but simply and gratefully took her. Kept her, too, for the longest while.

One-Eye didn't stumble in on their twisting trysting, but the secrets of the town beneath the Colonel's gaze were few. One-Eye took note, as spring persisted into hothouse summer, that Annalise wasn't doe-eyed sad as much, and further, that she ceased her seeking of my favor, went the other way in less than coy avoidance. He nosed around with two and two, but kept on reaching five. Still, he persisted and, by deduction more than any other way, reached summary conclusion of true correctness that Annalise was having an affair. Annalise did not deny it when, at last, he sought a confrontation.

Who?

None of your business, who, she said.

I think it is, Anna, he said. You've had a lot of lead rope for your years. Maybe much too much.

Too late for holiness.

Is it Andrew? Wynn?

None of your business who.

One-Eye lost his temper at this guarded confirmation, his mind a jumble at the memory of the plea he'd made one stormy, deadly midnight long ago. Annalise stood to flee. One-Eye grabbed her sparrow wrists and forced her back into her chair. Her eyes reddened at the pain, but she would not cry at him.

It isn't any *boy*, she said, spitting out the final word with angry scorn.

Then who? he hissed, sorry even as he spoke, the answer known. Then who?

His voice trailed off, diminished of its fire, and she told him.

. . .

The blunt-edged spike pierced several hearts, though words of final recrimination were few. One-Eye and Wylie had a scene, but One-Eye's steam was gone, deflated by the knowledge that while Wylie's deed was truly vile, the blame and guilt were shared by many. One-Eye quit our operation—the least of gestures possible—and took his tools to the Tatums, there, in time, to tutor Wynn, and leaving me the single heir to *Thunder Too*.

Although no further words were ever spoken, the silent knowledge of the liaison drove yet another wedge between the members of the Mavis household. We three— Wylie, Miss Ma, and I—lived our sunup-sundown days in isolation anyhow, each burdened by a host of dark secrets and black thoughts. This was simply one more curtain round our hard and burdened souls.

What Wylie gained by all of this I didn't know, could only guess. Release? A comfort unavailable in other ways, from other souls? Yes, no. And for Annalise, a gesture of defiance? A thrill? Escape? Yes, no. Her Wylie, so I felt, could have been anybody. Denied me by my pursuit of other charms, did she take Wylie to strike a glancing blow at me, to take from me the final part of what I'd never had? Was *I* to blame?

She was a little girl who grew up without her mother, said One-Eye, and with a father who was away a lot.

When did she find out about Mae? I asked.

One day when she was nearly five, he said. I remember

it was summer, and she would start to school that coming fall. We were having supper.

Daddy, can I have a mommy someday? she asked.

She voiced the question without tears or sadness, One-Eye told me. She was simply asking for something she thought she ought to have because everybody else had one. She might as well have been asking for a puppy or a new dress:

Daddy, can I have a mommy someday?

You have a mommy, One-Eye said, but she's dead.

Up to then, One-Eye had never talked to her about the accident, nor were there any pictures of Mae in the house. But since she'd asked, and for his benefit as well as hers, he told her nearly everything. He got a photo album and showed Annalise pictures of him and Mae when they were courting, and of their wedding day. That night he put a big picture of him and Mae in Annalise's bedroom. Later he heard his daughter cry, and went to see. Annalise asked him for a smaller picture of Mae, wallet-size.

Sure, honey, One-Eye said. What do you want it for?

Pillow.

One-Eye looked at me, and then beyond.

That picture never left her, he said. I wouldn't be surprised if it's with her even now.

CHAPTER
16

There was another seduction of a Mavis, that selfsame summer of my eighteenth year, no less surprising than the first, no less doomed to short-lived brilliance. Like Annalise, Betsy Potter was a beauty, though of a very different sort. Austere, aloof, she held her beauty close, as well as her charms. She wore no flashy dresses, she cut her hair benignly short, and while she took a joke as well as any—raising her glasses and her eyebrows in giggly appreciation of the verbal tickle—I always felt she'd be hard-pressed to tell one. A librarian, cut and dried, she'd be, if once she gathered up her gumption to leave Four Corners and find a city with a library. I carried her books through school corridors, walked miles beside her, talked hours beneath the Colonel's gaze. To her and her alone—who else?—I tossed my dreams and fears, my loves and hates. She caught them all, returned them all, each bound in new and brilliant wrapping.

But though our closeness grew, our passion was a one-way street, much to my tender dismay.

One white-hot suffocating day in August we packaged up a picnic basket, and in my hot-rod Ford we set out to the north.

It's going to be a corker, she said, a glint of perspiration forming on her upper lip.

I nodded agreement, offered her a flask, which she accepted, let the bitter burning trickle down her throat. And likewise I. North we drove at satisfying speed along the asphalt highway, enclosed on either side by parched and dusty brambles, and let the sticky hum of tires fill our ears. We joined the blue and hazy mountains and felt a gentle cooling as we began to climb. North of Gaffney, a silent hamlet, I turned onto a dusty, rutted road. We bounced and jounced in silence, until we reached a clearing. There, the rude road ran out into cool and grassy parking lot. We were on a small plateau. We heard the hidden whispering of the distant falls. Loading up our picnic things, we descended a steep and narrow trail, but one whose steps by untold generations had been carved to the precise dimensions of a staircase.

Soon we reached the bottom of the trail, unpacked, and stood in awe of that which lay before us. The Quahill Mountains were granite mounds of dullish blue and hazy gray, save at this one cathedral place where a narrow horseshoe falls had long ago unearthed a lost remain of iron ore. The horseshoe opened to the west and slightly south, so that the lowering sun of imminent sunset bathed the stone behind the water's torrent in a brilliant, sparkling crimson, not unlike the pictures I had seen of splashing, sequined cabaret singers, floodlit-bright. Between us and the distant falls, a swimming hole, a deep blue pool of water, nearly still, of mystery depths. This, then, was Fiery Tongue, a place well known to all but rarely visited in its isolation.

We were alone. We spread a blanket, stripped down to our bathing suits, sipped the lively whiskey, nibbled, talked of people in our lives, now so distant, faraway. The sun and the slow roar of the falls melted all concerns, save one that would not yield.

Wylie is a strange, strange man, I said as if to dream. I don't want to be like him.

Why do you have to be? Betsy pondered, lying back, her slender toes playing with the cool green grass at blanket's edge.

I feel drawn to him in ways I don't understand and don't much like, I said. He's not evil. He's not even particularly mean, yet he keeps hurting people. He's hurt Miss Ma, and me, and . . . he's hurt nearly everyone he's touched.

Is that the part of him you're drawn to?

I don't know.

I can't imagine, she said, lifting on one elbow. *You*'re not evil. You're just about the kindest, nicest, sweetest boy I've known. I'm glad you're not going to get mixed up in all that racing.

What makes you think I'm not? I asked.

You haven't yet.

Doesn't mean I won't. I like working on Wylie's cars.

What do you like about beating out an old fender so your mean, evil daddy can go run it up somebody's tail-pipe? Betsy teased, knowing she could get away.

There's a lot of satisfaction helping build a car that runs fast, runs smooth, stays together for a hundred laps. You haven't seen much racing, but there aren't many cars out there like that. Maybe Spencer's, is all.

So what's the problem? asked Betsy, her face so close to mine I could feel her whiskey-sweetened breath.

I sat up abruptly.

The problem, I said, is that I've seen what it takes to go to the big time, even if I don't drive. I don't want to spend my life in Four Corners. Got to get out, see what's there.

You think Wylie should have done that?

Maybe, maybe not. If he had, maybe he'd be dead by now.

Andrew!

Oh, relax, Bets. I didn't mean it that way. It's just there's a lot of fast company on the Circuit. Maybe Wylie couldn't have handled himself up there as good as he can down here.

Wylie's good, isn't he?

Good and mean. What he and Clyde got into last year was fine, sort of. God, I could have died when Miss Ma slapped old Clyde up aside his knee. I thought he'd pass out from the shock of it. But that stuff with Spencer a few years back was uncalled for.

So why did you defend him when Wynn came running?

I dunno. Instinct? If I wasn't his blood I'd have turned my back on the son of a bitch for sure, or jumped in on Clyde's side. That's what frightens me the most: not that Wylie's my daddy, but that I'm his son.

A pause. A strong, warm breeze luffed through the cathedral, swishing leaves and bending grasses. I turned on my stomach, away from Betsy, lost.

Do you know about Wylie and Annalise? I asked, my eyes closed.

Yes, was her careful reply.

Guess everybody does.

Pretty much.

Do you think it's terrible, Betsy, what's going on?

No, I don't.

You don't? I blurted, genuinely startled.

No, I don't. I like Annalise. That may come as a shock, but I do. And so does everybody else who's ever met her.

I like her, too, I defensed. Christ, though, I can't look her in the eye because Wylie's screwing her, but I like her. That's not the point.

It's not far off. I like Annalise and I respect her. Feel sorry for her, somewhat. She's got too much energy and vitality for Four Corners. It comes out in unusual ways, sometimes. God, I watched her put on makeup once. You know how long she took?

Couldn't begin, I said.

Forty-five minutes. Eek!

Indeed.

She wants out. She's after affection—someone to lean on and to care for her. One-Eye's had it rough, I guess, but he hasn't been the best poppa in the world. Does he ever talk about Anna?

Never . . . A little.

He should—about her and to her. He'd find out some things.

Like what?

Like number one, began the Betsy lecture, Wylie didn't seduce Annalise any more than Annalise seduced him. Like number two, one real good reason Annalise went at Wylie is because you, Andrew, more or less shut her out. Number three, if your eyes were open, you'd see the relationship has no future. It'll last until somebody or something shows her the ticket out of town, no more. And going back to number two, I'm very, very glad.

What? . . . Oh . . . Glad of what?

Glad you cold-shouldered Annalise.

Really? I popped.

Really, Betsy murmured. Whiskey-sweet close again, she brushed her lips against my neck hairs, suddenly attentive.

I twitched, bedazzled by the shock, confused by the sudden turning of the one-way passion street. Numbly drunk, my head twice-filled with singing, spangled hummingbirds, I passed the overture. Instead, I stumbled insecurely down to water's edge, walked out the sloping rocky bottom to reach the place, waist-high now, where it fell off sharply to its bottomless bottom—at least, I had never touched the bottom of its deepest part. I swam smartly to the middle of the pool, agog, delighted at my sudden rise to grace—if that, in fact, was what had happened. I did not know, for sure. I did not care.

I swam back to near the shore, treaded water as I slipped out of my swimming suit, balled it up, and threw it landward.

Andrew! Betsy said, the second time that day.

Come in, I shouted. Take your suit off. Come in.

Somebody will see.

Nobody will see. Hurry on.

Betsy slowly stood and made the water's walk, and slowly, smiling still, she pulled the shoulder straps of her suit, revealing one fine breast and then the other.

More, I laughed. Much more.

She shimmied the suit down beyond her hips and knees and let it loudly crash to the rocks below. With one arm over her chest and a hand to hide her groin, she picked her way on the awkward rocks until the water was deep enough for her to glide swimmingly into the pool's blue depths. She dog-paddled to my side. We played, she and disbelieving I, touching and caressing.

Don't be so grabby, she said, diving low to grab me by the balls.

I looked away toward the thundering, towering falls. Off to one side was a narrow ledge at the water's edge. I pulled myself out. Using narrow foot- and hand-holds, I climbed to a second ledge perhaps ten feet higher and dived, cutting the water with no more ripple, I could tell, than a knife. Betsy Potter, my cool, aloof librarian-to-be—whoo-boy—tried similarly, but could not muster strength to pull herself to the initial ledge. I moved to help her, pushing mightily on her tensed and dimpled fanny, but could not myself obtain the necessary leverage to push her up. We fell back splashing, caught in awkward embrace.

Soon the frolic slowed and we turned to other matters, while our watery universe drew narrower and narrower. I turned stiff and, wide-eyed joyful, guided Betsy's hand to my erection.

Goodness, she smiled, sputtering.

I, in turn, touched her, and felt a slippery wetness. Without coyness, she opened her legs and we attempted to couple, sinking below the surface of the water.

Is this possible? asked Betsy at a bobbing emergence from below.

I don't know, I said with honesty. Let's find out.

It was no easy task, all that, required great patience, great dexterity. But Betsy finally was able to receive me. By paddling with one hand and clutching with the other, we amazed ourselves with good and cheery tingling. Thus we stayed joined, moving rhythmically in the water and often beneath it, bursting to the surface to catch the air.

Now? I questioned.

Betsy bobbed goofy assent.

Take a deep breath, I said. Hang on.

Betsy locked her arms around my shoulders, her legs behind my knees. With both hands I held her buttocks, and thrusting and receiving, thrusting and receiving, we sank and tumbled, nearly free of gravity's hold, through the cool cleansing, until we hit a chilling layer of water unwarmed by summer's sun. Once more I thrust, and twice, felt Betsy's pulsing, and knew of my release. Thus bonded, we fell apart and to the surface shot, with bursting lungs.

Goddamn, I said while swimming circles, gasping air.

My puss'll leak for two days straight, said Betsy, sated, floating on her back.

A sudden yelp from her.

Oh, my God, she said. Look up there.

I raised my eyes to where she pointed, at an overlook atop the falls. There a man sat on his haunches. Overalled and whiskey-hatted, smoking, he stared from bramble shadows at the pool and its recently conjugal water bugs.

How long do you think he's been there? Betsy asked.

No telling, I said. We're not the first to swim here bare-butt. He probably likes a little thrill, is all.

What do we do?

Not much to do. Be modest. Look friendly.

You're joking.

We paddled, even mustered up a slight wave in the direction of the stranger's towering perch. He left. We dashed for shore. We talked of leaving then ourselves, declined the thought, and waited with our whiskey and our foodstuff for the lateness of the sun and the crimson sparkle of Fiery Tongue.

A sadness came to me—to us—and from my Betsy, now, a curious question.

Are you afraid of dying? she asked from far away.

No, I'm not, I said. I'm not afraid of death or dying, though at the race track I've seen plenty others make the brutal trip. I used to be afraid—terrified. Miss Ma, when asked, said only that it's a gentle passage, like sleep, and when you wake you'll be with God and angels and all who've predeceased you. No help, that. At times I've been afraid to go to sleep, or even shut my eyes. I'm not talking years ago, but very recent history. I was so afraid of sleep that I would do anything to stay awake—read, think, work unnecessary hours on the race car. Eventually I did fall asleep, of course, but bathed in sweat, soaked through from the exertions of trying to stay awake, to stay alive.

Betsy's eyes remained averted. She pulled the blanket to her waist and nibbled at a sweet-stemmed grass.

While I did not believe that I would meet the angels, I continued, neither did I totally disbelieve, either. What I came to realize, one soft afternoon last fall, it was, when the dying sun threw golden beams across the glade in which I found myself, was that I could not ever hope to know. Like all others, I would have to wait my turn to find such answer. So, why worry? Why even think about my death, or dying? Why confound myself? In now or later time I would be privy. Then would be the moment for such thoughts, not before. And—*snap*—just like that I ceased my morbid contemplations, save for one.

Which is?

Is this, I rambled on. One persistent thought still wanders in and out. It's sort of weird, a strange idea of multiple, coexistent physical realities.

I beg . . .

Listen, listen. Think of all the vast and empty space

between the stars, and in relation the awesome voids between the spinning particles of a single atom. We live in a physical world governed by a strict, unbending set of physical laws. What if . . . What if, when we die, we pass from this world into yet one more, governed by another set of laws, unknown, unseen, unfelt by us, but equally valid? And if one more, why not two or three, or more, until infinity? Strange, I know, but strangely comforting. The shorthand of it is this: maybe the dead, from their internal inspection, don't really die at all, but keep right on existing within the boundaries of their newfound world. In other words, maybe Mae Rivers and Jason Martin, for examples, still live, by their accounting, are only dead to those they've left behind.

Andrew Mavis, you believe in ghosts and angels both.

Maybe I do, I said. I tried this out on One-Eye once, for curiosity. He thought the matter through.

Maybe my Mae didn't die after all, he said, that nighttime long ago. Maybe *I* did. Another inch or two, either way, and I would have, that's for sure. Maybe I am real only to myself.

Betsy and I played and fondled till the time of dying, dancing sun, created aching sadness once again, and left that quiet place.

We ascended the staircase trail of stone and saw the car, its left-rear tire flat. As I changed it, I found the source—a slash that could only have been made with a knife.

Why did he do that? Betsy asked.

I'm more curious why that's all he did do, I said, sensing that the memory of the day's perfection would linger scarred, forever.

CHAPTER
17

The new alliances thus formed, by passion's lively wanderings and racing's fickle hand, should have brought a grand excitement to the next few years. But they did not. Instead, the opposite. With such predictability did matters leaven out that by the time of my maturity plus one—the year was 1962—the air was stale, heavy, dead with unrequited resolution. The calm, so false, was of the kind that precedes summer thunderstorms and embraces giant armies on the eve of awful battle. No cannon rumbled from the heights, but down below, the pickets kept their powder dry in anticipation of engagement.

With One-Eye's cool persuasion, Wynn took to racing and progressed with ease, his heart and instincts more than making up for errors of style and technique. I maintained Wylie's cars with excellent results—if I may say—kept up with all the latest speed-trick fads, and added notions of my own. At the centerpiece, as always, was the unresolved dispute between Wylie and Spencer. While neither chose to accelerate their silent conflict, neither did they move to exorcise the tensions. Their ancient feud had settled to a wary neutrality, there to ossify and harden. The ghostly, misty furies converged, took stations, waited.

Heyward Scrivens felt pressure of a different sort. The whiskey trade fell off precipitously, due mainly to the legislative wetting of the state, and closer home, his bullring speedway fell victim to a sudden patronage decline.

The reason was Wylie. He was winning too much. In the oppressive season under note, he reeled eight straight wins at Four Corners. Add to that a trio from the year before, and by September the fluky streak was at eleven. The competition, mad at first, grew discouraged. Then mad again and discouraged again in a second cycle. Spencer, with the skill to challenge but not the killer instinct, took his peaceful seconds; Wynn, with juices for the hunt but not yet owning all the skills, flailed his car and wore his patience, gaining nothing. And save for Tatums two, Heyward's whorish bullring might as well have been devoid of other race cars. In consequence, the fans, at first intrigued by such a Wylie victory skein, grew tired at the stale sameness and showed their ultimate displeasure—by staying home.

Wylie and I still maintained his successive *Thunder Toos* at the stall in Heyward's mill, which is where Heyward found us not three nights after number eleven was cleanly locked away. Damn mad Heyward hadn't even presented Wylie with his victory-circle check or trophy. At the payoff shack, he counted out the winning purse and laid it flat, almost daring Wylie to take it.

Wylie did.

Now Heyward poked his head in through the door.

Mind if I come in? he asked.

Course not, Wylie said, not looking up. It's your door, your shop. Make yourself at home.

Nice run, Saturday night, Heyward said.

You didn't seem to think so at the time. Got lucky.

Aaw, Wylie. I had my mind on other things. No offense.

None taken. I just noticed, is all.

Heyward snubbed out his short cigar in an old hubcap, scratched his gleaming head.

You've won a lot, Wylie, he said. Eleven in a row's impressive, in any league.

Mmm.

But it turns people off, sometimes. They like to see the underdog win every now and then, and want to feel the others have a fighting chance.

Everybody's got the same chance. My car's clean. I play inside the rules—ask Andrew, here—as much as anybody.

Course you do. How can I complain if you're zeroed in?

Guess maybe you can't.

Still, this is the first season since I opened that I've lost money on the speedway.

Sorry to hear that, said unmoved Wylie.

You and I have been straight with each other, Wylie. Agreed?

Agreed.

Then I'll be straight now. It would be good for business if Spencer or some of the other boys won a race, now and then.

Not for my business it wouldn't.

Wylie turned, faced Heyward for the first time. I,

working on an engine suspended from a portable hoist nearby, also turned Heyward's way.

I lost a car in Ashley Oaks last month and tried to lose me another in Terminus last week, Wylie said. Look at that.

He pointed to a car in the corner of the room that had been squashed so low there was barely room to look out. The rollover had been brutal, violent.

If it wasn't for Four Corners, Wylie continued, this would be a very mediocre season for old Wylie Mavis. I'm much obliged.

Heyward hesitated. The furies waited; soon now, soon. Heyward next took off his sunglasses, a gesture I thought theatrical, but one to indicate some serious action. He blinked, squinted, from his pocket drew a bulging envelope.

I was hurt to hear of your trouble at Terminus, he said, looking square at Wylie's hard, unblinking eyes. This here should cover the repairs.

He offered the greenback bribery bulge to Wylie.

Generous of you, Heyward, Wylie said. But Andrew and I can get it back to where it was by beating and banging on it some. Looks worse than it is.

You're refusing this? thin-lipped Heyward asked.

Better than that, I'll forget you were here tonight. Andrew will, too.

Heyward stood, said nothing right away, withdrew the envelope, returned it to his pocket and his sunglasses to his eyes. He looked slowly from Wylie to me and back, and back to me.

I thought you might, he said. No hard feelings. By the way, I'll be needing this space for some machinery I've got coming in. No rush to leave. Two weeks ought to be sufficient time.

Sooner than that, said Wylie, if there's need.

Two weeks is fine.

Heyward clicked his heels, turned, and found the exit door.

The try for number twelve was an ordinary race, a Saturday nighttime two-hundred-lapper notorious only for the flyby dust. Heyward had let up on his maintenance, and his track had ceased to be a bullring gemstone. The stands were less than half capacity, and in the pits an equal unenthusiasm held. The field was small, a dozen cars, no more. Spencer, just by looking, had set himself to run a second, and by a similar glance I knew that bloodhound Wynn would make a chase, then heighten One-Eye's work load by a crumpled fender, maybe more.

Wynn threatened his car to qualifying fastest. Wylie lazed to fifth, and Spencer seventh. But when the green flag dropped, Wylie waited but two laps before he took the lead, ho-hum, and built his margin to a lap and more near the race's dulling midpoint. A slender spin by one whose name I can't recall brought out a yellow at ninety-seven laps. The field slowed, then one by one the cars churned for the pits and a tanking up. Uncle Julian was my crew that night, as he occasionally would do if thunder road was quiet. Wylie pitted. Julian handed me a gas can, and I labored hard to lift the unwieldy torpedo to the angle that would permit the nozzle to enter Wylie's tank. Julian checked the tires all around for cuts or stones, pronounced them fit.

On the restart lineup, Wylie led the scraggly pack, Spencer tucked in second, a lap and more behind, and Wynn was in the lineup seventh.

Wylie jumped the starter's flag by half a lap, a master's stroke, and left the field behind him save for Spencer, no starting slouch himself. And so the two roared past the flag together, Wylie high and Spencer on his bumper, two proud and ancient warriors locked together for another red-dust go-around. Indeed, so thick was the soft and swirly dust that the next events were rendered almost invisible.

As Wylie neared the first-turn entrance, he, without a warning, dived low to the inside of the race track. Spencer, next behind, was already turning, one groove lower. He stood the brakes, but late, too late, and cranked his steering wheel rightward, catching Wylie in the left-rear quarter-panel. Soon the cars were locked together in an eerie red-dust mating dance—Wylie, pointed to the infield and sliding farthest down the track, nearest turn one, and Spencer, pointed outside, sliding opposite—their side-by-saddle cars reversed, drivers' sides together. They could have reached out and shaken hands. Both cars, together, moved for the outside rail in the middle of the turn. Spencer hit the rail head-on, bounced backward, and slithered down the banking, off the track. A second after Spencer's smash, rear-end Wylie did the same, a ton. In the building tangle I saw the front end of the car lift well up off the ground at the instant of the impact, saw Wylie, hanging on with all his angry might, look to his left—thus, back up the track toward four.

The flagman didn't wait for cues. He waved the yellow for seconds only, then grabbed the red to signal that the track was blocked and all the cars should stop.

Wynn never slowed. He never even lifted. He T-boned Wylie, hung up there unmoving, as surely as if the spot had been surveyed. I started running for the turn, with One-Eye close behind, and many others. Some accidents you can tell. Maybe ions in the air march chorus-line a certain way; don't ask me how.

159

Spencer was okay. Even as I dashed my dash, he chugged hard across the track for Wynn, unbuckled him and helped him through the window. Wynn's knees collapsed and he fell toward the ground until impeded by Spencer's mighty arms. He was groggy coo-coo, but I knew he'd be just fine.

Wylie was imperfect. The left side of his car was concave. His roll cage held, but barely, and Wylie slumped, his head and chest half hanging out the window. I thought he'd started searching for new realities. Blood was everywhere, sticky, sickly. An oil fire lurched to life beneath the car, its harbinger a thin and delicate strand of dark and ugly smoke. Quickly One-Eye and I, with several others' help, got Wylie out and carefully, carefully laid him on the ground beside his car. His left arm angled at a point between his shoulder and his elbow. His left-leg pants were torn. I saw his left-leg kneecap pushed to the outside of his knee.

From the distance I heard the wailing of a siren. One-Eye checked Wylie's pulse, nodded that he'd found one, fast but strong. There were no surges of blood that I could see. Impossible it was to guess at what had happened inside elsewhere. The siren drew nearer, groaned in stopping. The ambulance attendants pushed and probed, then bundled Wylie on a stretcher. Wylie moaned. Perhaps ten minutes had passed. I got in beside him. The ambulance moved on out, bouncing across the no more dry-slick track. Wylie moaned again and spoke in whispers, but I heard him, brought the ambulance to a halt, got out, and walked back again across the track. The ambulance roared off.

One-Eye, Heyward, Julian stood in a little cluster by themselves.

He gonna be okay? asked Heyward.

Don't know, I said, burning daggers at him.

Tell Miss Ma what happened, I said in Julian's direction. Bring her to the hospital.

When I could, I motioned One-Eye off to where we'd be alone.

Wylie says to stay with the car and lock it up somewhere, I told him, who raised an eyebrow, arched the other. That's all he said, One-Eye. He said not to let anybody else but you and me touch that car, and to lock it up.

He didn't say why? asked One-Eye.

No. He said only what I said he said, and to trust only you.

My voice was harsh and hard, though I really didn't mean for it to be. My eyes were dry, as I knew they would be, once this moment came.

Behind our house there was a one-stall garage, seldom used. One-Eye and I gathered the remains of Wylie's car, no easy task, so scattered and deformed it was, and towed it there. I knew there'd be no reconstruction of this particular *Thunder Too*. I feared there might be no rebuilding Wylie.

I put the car under bolt-lock key, and with One-Eye rode in silence to the hospital. The black air was dusty-hot. Clothes stuck to skin and hair plastered foreheads. Oppressive stillness ruled, the quiet broken only by the crickets' strident twir. So this, I thought, is where and how the furies chose to strike.

Miss Ma was at the door.

Room 217, is all she said, and left.

One-Eye and I followed at some distance along a porcelain-bright, green-fluorescent corridor, pausing briefly, undetected, at the entrance to a lounge where certain of our cast had gathered. There, a voice I knew to be the ambulance attendant's told his tale to Heyward and Uncle Julian.

The son of a bitch is amazing, he said. Shock is a wonderful thing—dulls the senses, numbs the pain—but it'll flat take you out if you don't watch after. I'm sitting next to him, half expecting him to croak on me right there, what with all the blood and his left arm and leg bent at all the wrong places, shouting and screaming at him not to lose consciousness. Wylie's lying there, eyes closed, silent, as pale as gray brick, as we roll along. And halfway here, about, he says in a loud voice:

Tell the bastard driving that if he clips one more curb or finds another pothole, I'm gonna get up and drive this thing myself.

Wylie'll be okay, the attendant rambled on. A little bent, but otherwise okay. It's a shame what those Tatums did to him, though. Took two of them to get at one of him. I guess the losers in the racing game can only take so much.

We took the stairs to the second floor and found his room. Miss Ma had gone inside. Bloodhound Wynn and disconsolate Spencer stood by themselves.

Andr . . . Wynn began.

I shut him off.

Where you been, One-Eye? Spencer asked.

One-Eye told them where, but didn't fully tell them why.

We could have used you, said Wynn.

I'm sorry.

People are talking that we ganged up on Wylie, Spencer said. I hope you don't believe that.

Damn, One-Eye, muttered Wynn, eyes averted from

my gaze. Wylie isn't my favorite person, but I'm not nuts enough to chop down my career to nail a piece of him. If I want Wylie, I'll get him tidier than that.

Before I could respond, or One-Eye, Miss Ma cracked the door and called me in. I took One-Eye with me.

Wylie's room was dim and spacious, austere, antiseptic. Miss Ma sat in one chair, One-Eye took another. Wylie lay in silence. Intravenous fluids ebbed and flowed. I stood and listened to a young, officious doctor run the list of Wylie's hurts. It was quite a list: a compound fracture of his left leg and ditto for his left arm, four broken ribs, one of which had punctured and collapsed his left lung and come within an inch of his fiercely beating heart, lacerations and contusions. With a certain prim satisfaction, the doctor announced that within twenty-four hours Wylie would be black-and-blue on his left side, more or less from head to foot.

How long will he be in the hospital? I asked, to interrupt the color show.

At least four weeks, the doctor said, depending on the extent of his internal injuries. We'll know when lab tests come back from Terminus.

He'll live, then?

Oh, yes, the doctor said again, a smile briefly passing by his lips. He's broken up, as I've just said, but there's no X-ray evidence of fractured vertebrae or damage to his spinal column.

He didn't break his back, then? Miss Ma interjected. Or his neck?

No.

How about his head? I asked. Did he go out? Is he under now?

If by his head you mean his brain, the doctor said as

I glowered, by all rights he should have suffered a massive concussion. But there's no evidence. We had to knock him out to do our work. What he needs most now is rest. He'll not be in a socializing mood for quite some time.

And later, when he leaves the hospital? One-Eye entered in.

The doctor stared hard.

Mr. Rivers, I believe? That's not a thing we have to worry on just now.

Tell us, I said in a voice I hoped would not permit dispute.

Throughout the body, the doctor lectured, there are nerves that control all sensation and mobility. In Mr. Mavis's left leg, those nerves are severed. He'll not have any feeling in a portion of that limb.

He'll be paralyzed, said Miss Ma.

He'll be able to walk, but he won't have control of his leg below a certain point.

He'll have a limp? I asked, annoyed with this building indirectness.

There'll be no limp, the doctor said. It will be more of a . . . drag, I'd think. With a walker, or a cane, perhaps, I imagine Mr. Mavis will be able to get around just fine. And with a brace, you might not even know.

Is this point of which you speak above or below the knee? I asked.

I'm afraid above.

Then he can't drive a race car, I said.

If you can put an automatic transmission in one, I'd see no reason.

The doctor left. We three stayed in Wylie's room for several hours more. The corridor emptied, as well the lounge, save for Uncle Julian and Aunt Melvina, who rounded up some thoughtful sandwiches and coffee. Around one o'clock, it must have been, Miss Ma told me to go home.

There's no use for everyone to stay, she said.

We left Miss Ma in vigil, old and strong.

Let's go back to *Thunder Too*, I said to One-Eye when we'd left Miss Ma's earshot, and see what we can see. I want to stare at that wreck while everything's still fresh in my mind.

You'll be a lot fresher with some sleep, protested One-Eye mildly.

Why was Wylie so insistent that we put the car under lock and key? I asked, ignoring him. What can that old wreck of a car tell us?

Just thinking out loud, One-Eye said, and pardon me for what I say. Your daddy's a mean s.o.b., but he's just about the smartest dirt-track driver I've seen. Now—just thinking, mind you—he made a mistake tonight. When's the last time he did that? Make a mistake you'd expect some yellow-bumper rookie to make—dropping low on a restart and chopping Spencer?

What's on your mind? I asked.

Nothing in particular. Just wondering what would cause a driver like Wylie to make a mistake.

Soon the short trip home was done.

The wreck was eerie in the flicker light from a swaying bulb that threw moving shadows to the darkened walls of the old garage.

Maybe something broke on the car, I said.

I'm thinking the same, One-Eye said. But what? What exactly did Wylie say to you?

He said to stay with the car, lock it up, and don't let anybody else but you near it. But given who you work for now . . .

Wylie and I were together for a long time, One-Eye said to cut the thought.

We disassembled *Thunder Too*, a job the accident made easier. Conclusions were impossible. The left-front wheel was cracked. No wonder. The oil lines were shredded. We toured the car, found nothing. I wasn't even sure what we were looking for. A bad part? Evidence? Of what?

Okay, again, said One-Eye. What exactly did Wylie do out there?

He dove to the inside, quickly, I said. Made a mistake . . . Unless . . .

Unless what?

Unless he knew he was in trouble, or about to be.

Fuel starvation? One-Eye asked of no one. When he punched the accelerator, he was okay for maybe two seconds, then felt the car settling. I'll bet that's what he tells us, when he can.

Anything can cause that, I said. Dust . . . there was a lot of dust. A sticky carburetor valve. A broken fuel line. A hundred things could have happened.

You're right, said One-Eye. Let's try to find the one.

We took apart the fuel system, from gas tank to carburetor. Everything was clean; everything intact. Nothing clogged, nothing dirty, nothing broken. It was, in fact, the only system in the car that had survived intact.

It was hot, I said. Maybe the fuel vaporized and he got vapor lock, felt as though the car was running out of gas.

Could be, One-Eye said with unconviction.

He removed the air filter and again looked inside the

carburetor, playing with his instincts. He rubbed his finger around the carburetor's innards.

Drain the gas tank, he said.

I did, into a clean washtub just outside the garage door.

Now mix it well and take a quart-glass jar and dip it full.

I did. We waited.

In five minutes, it was clear that there were two fluids in the jar, layered like a fancy drink.

There's your answer, he said. The top is gas; the bottom, I think we'll find, is water. At least, I surely hope so.

With that, One-Eye carefully skimmed the top, then dropped a lighted match into what remained.

Nothing happened.

Transfixed, I squatted, joining One-Eye, who had risked the other in the proving of his hunch. Like two Indians round the dying embers of a fire, we watched the thin plume of smoke dance to dissipation, the true and final evidence of Wylie's keen suspicion.

CHAPTER 18

. . . A rifleshot of agony shatters my knees, overriding all other pain. I am tumbling still—that much I know—but points of reference now are lost. My eyes stay closed, denying me a visual fix, and the turbulent madness dulls my body gyroscope to incoherent babbling. Whether I am up or down, sideways port or starboard, I know not, only that I'm rolling still, with diminishing awareness and concern. I grasp for any hold, find none that lasts; am amazed in an out-of-body way that I can even function thusly, so low my consciousness.

Then there's silence. The motor's dead at last. Surely, now, it's over, done with, surely. But no, I tumble still and hear the viperous hiss of metal on the grass, more shattering of parts, muffled now, as though a heavy blanket has been tossed across this heaving miscarriage. Another silence, then. And then another hiss and muffled crumbling. I'm flying through the air, then bouncing, taking off. How high? How far? How long must this go on?

The mess of which I am a part feels lighter than before,

its inertia slashed by some significant portion. I blink, blurred and hazy, losing focus, and realize with calm detachment that my car's been shorn in half. The monster engine of my transport is there no more, ripped from its mount by rail impact or bouncing, I cannot tell. Not only is the engine gone, but nothing remains forward of the dashboard and the fire wall. My tortured, beastly beauty has come unhinged.

Again the grassy hiss. The black box, Andriotti's measure of my race car's worth, and mine, slams into my neck. I hardly notice. I smell the grass for one brief notch of time. I claw at it, foolishly, I realize, desperate to make contact with some solid object.

Will this end? Ever end?

Another silence. I tense for further impact, but the silence stays, at last. It is over.

How bad?

I struggle to breathe. My mouth opens, slack-jawed, but no sound emerges. I feel the onset of a bleak descent. I cannot let this happen. I must get out. I cannot lose consciousness. I struggle to hear, but receive the black silence of the tomb, or womb. I must get out. There's fire, surely. The smoke I'd smelled before—surely there must be fire. I feel none, smell none.

I am exhausted. My breath comes in shallow pants and blows. I want to lie down in the green grass, feel its rich, soothing coolness. I want to dream a mindless dream. I want to see the heaving dogwood blooms, rich and lush and white. I want to lie down by a mountain brook and let cool air soothe my raw-rubbed skin. My eyes are heavy.

I cannot lose consciousness; must not. I struggle to open my eyes, but cannot see. A red haze fills them. I cannot move my limbs, so heavily is each one weighted. I cannot hear. There's a ringing in my ears that builds and builds as if to implode my skull. I smell. I smell the pungent odors of gasoline and rubber, singed oil, tarnished grass.

The pain . . . the pain! Thank God for that. The dull ache begins somewhere down below and spreads with tempered certitude through every layer of my body. I try to isolate components, assess the damage, but the dull and brutal achiness overrides the isolates. The pain builds by throbbing layers, each one greater and more enveloping than the one before, the epicenter somewhere deep inside my gut, in a place beyond my comprehension.

And then the pain starts slowly to subside, in layers, once again, like the peeling of an onion. I struggle to feel the pain, but it continues to subside. I must not let go of the pain. I cannot yield.

By force of will, by focusing on each and every trauma hurt, I retain my contact with consciousness. I must not yield.

I am upright; that much I know. By some perverse design the pinball game I've played has pitched me back into my driving seat. My helmet's there atop my head. I'm slumped forward, my right cheek on the steering column. I cannot see; I cannot move.

From a hollow distance far, I hear a siren, and like a drowning, flailing seaman I grasp the siren's call. 'Tis music to my ears; don't let it go. Do not.

The siren draws near, though far away still.

How bad?

In the same hollow tunnel there are voices.

There's no fire, says Bent Nose, his voice tinny, hollow, faraway. That's a miracle.

A real mess, says Red Face, his voice tinged with awe.

He's broken his harness. He ought to have been thrown out up there where the engine landed.

Might have been a better deal for him if he had.

Maybe not.

Look at his legs, bent up under that way.

For chrissakes, I think. *Do something*.

His eyes are open, says Bent Nose.

He grabs me by a dangling wrist.

He's not dead, he says.

My eyes are open? I think. *I cannot see.*

Get him out, comes a sharp command.

The voice is One-Eye's. I struggle to move, make words, but nothing happens. Nothing moves; no sounds emerge.

Get him out, says One-Eye once again. Gently boys, now, gently.

Bent Nose—or is it Red Face?—grabs me firmly beneath my arms and twists my body gently. He's done this more than once before. The other's arms work with my legs—but I feel no pain—and straighten me. One-Eye—this I know—removes my helmet and places his worn hands beneath my head.

Gently boys, now, gently.

I yield. I feel the brilliant sun. Darkness descends. I struggle no more, and sleep.

PART THREE

CHAPTER
19

How bad?

There's a not-unfriendly stillness to the sun-drenched, hollow air; no sign that reaches me of doom and gloom. Cautious voices wander quiet, no doubt assaying damages to man and car. How long was I out? Not long, by all the meager filtered signals I absorb. I cannot move my limbs. My wiry torso's numbed to dullness. My only contact with the pain is in my eyes, though crimson darkness is all I see. My eyes I flicker left and right, but each direction offers blitzkrieg shooting pain, a hammer's sullen blow, and even this I cease. I lie there waiting, wondering, once-removed from what must surely be a carnage scene.

What is going on?

I drift.

. . .

Once . . . Once, I found myself in Wylie's car, the two of us, alone. It was the middle of the night, the time for mournful torch songs and a goofy effort just to stay awake. This was after Wylie's crunch, and behind us in the narrow darkness swayed a flatbed loaded up with my race car, not his—a switch of things I had not yet grown used to, though by then I'd driven hard the bullring circuit for a time. The hour was late and sleepy. The road was ours alone. Dim dashboard lights threw excess creases in his craggy, stubbled face. His eyes, no longer racer's eyes, were soft and even mellow, and quite abruptly he began a song. No singer he, the words made rumbling, off-key passage, filled our tiny car atonally.

My heart knows, he sang with treacherous sadness. He sang:

> *My heart knows what the wild goose knows*
> *And I'm not going where the wild goose goes*
> *Wild goose, brother goose, which is best?*
> *A wandering soul, or a heart at rest?*
> *Fly away, fly away, fly away . . .*

Over and over he sang this song, as though he had found in it the expression of his inarticulate rage. Over and over he sang the words as we sped through the exhausted darkness, did not cease this song of his until the bleak first light of dawn returned him from the lost and mournful place he'd been.

• • •

I hear stilted conversations, far away, the words resonating tinnily.

Goddamn, says one I know is Bent Nose. God*damn*. Where's the chopper? Where?

One-Eye—it must be he—pulls Bent Nose from the scene and shushes him from speaking further in my presence. I smell tawny Annalise. Her perfumed makeup targets her an easy olfactory mark. She sniffles, sobs, her once-prolific, grand indifference broken. Bloodhound Wynn, from him a silence.

Here's the box, shouts Red Face from a distance. I found it up the track a way. It looks intact.

Good, I think. What will its readout tell? I hope it will exonerate me from the blame, though there's a doubt. It might, however, tell the dapper Jean-Pierre what he needs to know of me and my reactions in the pinch. I wonder: Did I pass his muster? Suddenly there's import to this thought. Did I pass? Would I earn the gofer's job, the trial for which has ended thusly? Hard to believe I've crunched a car, and me, for the privilege of such employment.

· · ·

Once . . . It was the eve of Wylie's funeral, less than a fortnight past, and Andriotti, silver-spleened, came by the house, an unexpected guest. He was, surprise, afraid. He chatted idly, offered Miss Ma comfort, coldly taken, and when alone with me revealed more.

I am never used to this, he said, his slender fingers held so tight that whiteness gleamed beneath his polished, bitten nails.

I raised an eyebrow, waited.

Are you afraid, Andrew, of what awaits us?

No, I said in honesty. Curious, for sure, but not afraid.

I didn't think so, he said. It's strange, for me. Even though I no longer drive, and therefore do not lose my friends with the frequency that once I did, I never miss a race-car driver's funeral, if I'm in the neighborhood. And I'm usually in the neighborhood. I wonder why.

Straightaway, he listed all the drivers he had known who now were gone—greats and near-greats, some; others, some, who never wore a garland; Wylie, now, to join them.

177

You're a survivor, I ventured, unsure of what he sought from me, if anything at all. You grin inside for having beat the rap.

Maybe, said Jean-Pierre. But why do we need another's mistake to remind us of our own good fortune?

Would you rather it had been your own? I smiled.

Wily Andrew, he said in unintended pun, and left.

· · ·

All decline to talk in my direction, or to touch.

It'll be here soon, says Bent Nose. I can hear it from afar.

How long's the flight? asks Jean-Pierre.

Ten minutes' time, no more, says One-Eye. They're ready for him at the hospital, have a team assembled.

And Miss Ma? asks Jean-Pierre.

I made the call, says One-Eye, though I could not bring myself to talk to her direct. His Uncle Julian has the news, and soon will be the one to take it to her house, and drive her down.

Ironies are building up, are due a fated clash with wry coincidence. Dear Uncle Julian. Dear mysterious Uncle Julian, bearing unknown demons of his own, is once again the designated harbinger of dirty tidings—he, who with an action twice removed, is the in-line cause of all our present trouble.

· · ·

Once . . . Once I owned a bike, my first and only, a pleasure craft created out of junk by One-Eye's master hand. It had no fenders and one gear only, and on the forks, both fore and aft, I clipped some plastic playing cards to zither loudly through the spokes. I loved that bike and rode it well.

One day near the square I spied young Annalise, not

178

yet tawny, still a buddy-chum. To show my prowess at the wheel, I sat myself atop the bars, back-facing, and pedaled furiously in adolescent show-off. I circled Colonel Stokes with mounting speed and confidence. The second time around I waved to Annalise with sanguine hopefulness.

Watch out! I heard the cry, but late, too late.

I bounced the cobbled curbing, lost my backward perch, and fell athunder at the Colonel's base, my head the first of me to strike.

I lay there coldcocked stunned, a gash of some dimension on my forehead trickling blood. By happenstance, it must have been, my fated Uncle Julian saw the fall, gathered up his nephew's tender wreckage, and bore me home to waiting Wylie and Miss Ma.

What the hell, said Wylie.

He's had a fall, said Uncle Julian. The cut's stopped bleeding. He'll be all right.

Angry Wylie grabbed me from his brother's arms so hard I thought he'd crush my ribs and carried me inside. Uncle Julian moved to follow in his wake, but Wylie slammed the door, denied him entrance though he'd only brought the message and hadn't had the smallest part in the doing of the deed.

But, Wylie . . . said my flustered uncle.

Slam. Goodbye.

• • •

One-Eye kneels close, at last, and whispers low, though he cannot be sure of my awareness.

We've called a helicopter for you, he says. Can you hear me, Andrew? Can you? That was quite a little number that you did, but you'll be at the hospital soon. Hang on for just a little longer. Hang on. Hang on.

I smell his breath, his sweat, and feel his fear. I try to

give a signal, but cannot. I hear a sound like moth wings beating.

Gently boys, now, gently.

. . .

Once ... But no. I sleep again, and wait.

CHAPTER
20

Who did it? I asked. Who had cause to try and kill Wylie?

We were still at the garage, staring at the thinly dancing plume of smoke and pondering all we'd just found out. One-Eye raised his head, exhausted, sad, and laughed a quiet, cynical laugh.

I don't think necessarily that anybody was trying to kill Wylie, he said. None come to mind who is brave enough or smart enough to figure a way to do him in, but there's a whole bunch of people who'd like to see him slowed down a little.

Who, One-Eye? Tell me.

Do your own list, he said. For starters, there'd be you and me.

Though weariness had finally made encroachment on my tired, muddled brain, I yielded to the slightest hint of smile.

Belief is everything, I said. There are some few things you've got to believe simply because if the opposite were true, you couldn't continue to function. I know *I* didn't do it. And no matter how badly Wylie once treated you, I cannot and therefore will not believe you capable of such an act. If I felt that of you—that you could kill, or hurt with such direct maliciousness . . .

Enough, he said, by way of closing that darkened, dusty corridor. You read me honestly, but there was once a time when in my heart I gladly would have revenged my daughter's fall. The moment passed, and no more need be said.

After Wylie gained assurances that he was going to live, a bandaged, splintered case but more or less intact, he yielded to the doctors' pleas and slept. There was talk of moving him to Terminus, but once the trauma crisis passed, Miss Ma and I agreed there was no real need.

Miss Ma brought flowers every day. From nine to six she kept the vigil in a straight-back chair, reading to herself or talking to Wylie in those few minutes of the hour when he was capable of some response. I checked in once or twice a day to ascertain his progress, and with One-Eye kept the early evening watch.

On about the tenth day, Wylie's racing eyes returned, glowed nuggets, mean as ever. The cuts about his face had not permitted shaving, and true to earliest predictions, his left-side body—those parts not enclosed by plaster cast or bandages—glowed ugly purple-blue. God, he was a picture mess.

What happened? Wylie asked in firm and parchy voice.

You had a bit of a shunt, One-Eye said in thin attempt at levity.

I know what the hell happened on the race track,

182

he said. What went wrong? Why'd the engine start to die?

You were right, Wylie, I said, trying to match his cold and brilliant stare. There was water in the gas tank. How'd you know?

I didn't know, for sure. I'd just never had an engine turn on me before, with such a vengeance. Are you sure of what you found?

I related all the searching One-Eye'd done, and I. There could be no mistake.

Wylie closed his eyes. I thought he'd nodded off, but no.

Who knows of this? he asked.

Everybody who wanted, saw us take the car and lock it up, I said. One-Eye and I, no others, are the only ones who know precisely what we found.

So the Tatums got revenge, he said.

Could have been, I said.

You aren't exactly the most popular man in the county, One-Eye said. Offhand, I could name you half a dozen who aren't disappointed to see you slowed.

Spencer has hated my guts for ten years and more, said Wylie. And that dumb-ass son of his is, well, a dumb ass.

Wynn isn't the brightest fellow of the lot, I said, but he isn't any kamikaze. He got knocked around pretty good himself, you know.

Wylie rambled on as though I hadn't said a thing.

We pitted next to each other, he said. I didn't have a hint of trouble until the restart, when we all gassed. It's a mess in those pits. You got to be a genius just to find them. Andrew, you filled me up, right?

I nodded.

You sure you used our gas can?

What are you saying, Wylie? asked One-Eye, angered. That your own son switched gas cans on you?

No, of course not, Wylie said. But there's a jillion people walking up and down the pits. Any one of them could do a switch. Who's going to check a gas can for what's inside? Gas, of course.

Spencer or Wynn'd have to be pretty damned sharp to pit their own car, jump out, switch cans, and jump back in without calling attention, I said.

Somebody could have done it for them, Wylie said. Like you say, it wouldn't be hard to find a willing soul.

There matters stayed. As predicted, Wylie was four weeks leaving the hospital. The date of his homecoming was first October. Unlike his previous return, so misty long ago, this one had no preparatory banners, no cast of friends and family. Miss Ma stayed home. One-Eye and I did the checkout, wheeled him down the green-tinged corridors to my waiting car. In the driveway of our house, One-Eye offered Wylie aid as he struggled to move from the front seat of the car to the wheelchair set up close beside it. Wylie refused all help, but with his left leg held by plaster and his left arm in a sling, not even Charlie Atlas could have gotten the necessary leverage. Wylie struggled endless minutes while One-Eye stood by helpless and I stared cold-eyed—unmoving and unmoved—as the little scene unfolded. Wylie showed no anger, no frustration, only ancient, prideful determination. Finally, soaked through by sweat though the autumnal day was crisp, he yielded.

Help me, he said.

We did. Inside the house, the talk was idle chatter, mostly racing. Much to Heyward's surprise, his crowds had fallen off even more with Wylie in the pasture, a note that gave Wylie more than mild satisfaction. We glanced upon the new and virile Circuit tracks—one and two and two and a half miles around, high-banked and fast—that had sprung up in the two and three past years, and how the racing sport was changing, Detroit-bankrolled by the millions.

Heyward's going to have to pave over his little race track here or close it up, said One-Eye. You see what lap speeds they're running on the biggest asphalt ovals? A hundred and seventy-five miles an hour, and more. And Terminus, I hear, is going to build a two-mile track. You think folks will come up here for rutted mud and dusty dirt if they can see this other kind of racing?

Wylie argued otherwise.

Look at those bankings, he said. There's a whole bunch of boys you're going to see retire pretty soon. Not everybody likes that speed, or driving round and round like bats hanging from the ceiling. Those bankings'll change your perspective on life, in a hurry. I don't guess I'll ever find out for myself, though.

He paused, leaned back, fatigued by such a monologue.

Maybe the fans will desert the dirt tracks, he said, but the drivers never will. But—when the fans go, so will the tracks. Still, it's no concern of mine. I'm done driving.

One-Eye offered protest. I did likewise, though I could not hide my insincerity.

No, Wylie said, it's over. I could rig the car up special, I suppose, and brace my leg the same, but by the time I figured all that out, there'd be no point. I sure can't run the Circuit at my age, and crippled, and it won't be long before the dirt stops paying money high enough to make it worth the while.

He paused again, surveyed the room: Miss Ma, One-Eye, and me.

Andrew, he said, it's time you learned to drive.

I blinked and nodded acquiescence to my destiny.

Yes, I said, it's time.

. . .

Once more aligned with Mavis blood, One-Eye again assumed the teacher's role, as he had with bloodhound Wynn two autumns to the past, and found, for sure, a different pupil from the one he'd had before. I certainly did not possess the natural talent that graced Wynn's driving. But this I knew, and did not try to go beyond the limits of my skill. Still, I was not hopeless and, indeed, made progress far faster than my modest optimism would allow. Two saving graces blessed my efforts. One was mechanical. I was quick and facile around a toolbox and had come to understand the way a race car worked to a degree I knew that Wynn could never hope to do. Not only could I tell my One-Eye what my car was doing, I could also offer thoughts as to the why of it and make corrections on my own. No small advantage, this. The other was a fierce and sullen concentration on the task at hand—witness my burned and blistered heel. If, to give a second example, I decreed a certain spot to be the place where I should lift the throttle and start the turn, then slowly I would work to gain that spot by tiniest of increments. But I would get there, soon enough.

Wynn, by comparison, approached the racing game all different. He'd go beyond that spot the first time out, spend anxious seconds gathering in his limit-bending car, then back it off a notch or two until he, too, had found it.

Slowly, I made progress. At the first, the excellence of my car, so strongly built by One-Eye's hand, gave me easy leverage over half the pack. Then I learned to pick my way beyond the middle class of cars and drivers, always careful to finish up a race and not leave One-Eye extra work to do.

This took some doing, but I had patience on my side, and inside twelve months' time or so, I found myself among the leaders now and then, much, I must admit, to my surprise, and even more to Wynn's.

And that is when the Mavis part of me gained dominance. While driving just to finish, I was antiseptic, clean—no Wylie-boiling blood to messy up the show. But when the possibility for checkers loomed, my genteel—all is relative—race-track personality flip-flopped, and I, like onetime Wylie, took affront at any car that dared to block my way. And more and more that car was bloodhound Wynn's, another twisting of the Mavis–Tatum rope.

Winning the race and racing to win aren't always part and parcel, a fact, like many others, that Wynn had failed to grasp. While he had found some checkered flags with which to decorate his walls, the creation of a race-track triumph was still a notch ahead of him. For me, to show the other hand, the winning was a thing I knew, though at the time of which I speak I'd yet to break my maiden.

The incident took place just shy one year of when I drove my first—and thus bare seven months ago: September '63. It was a slapjack hundred-lapper at Four Corners, one of those sloppy nights when nothing worked for either Wynn or me. Wynn and I were running hard together for fifth or sixth, his engine sour from the start and my car handling like a sled. Frustrated and tired with the wrestling of our slow, unwieldy steeds, we came through three and four together. Wynn sputtered, slowed a notch, and I, my car a dancing dervish with a headstrong mind its own, leaned on him. *Wham*. And leaned again. *Bam*.

187

I went bonkers, plain and simple, cannot tell it otherwise, and Wynn, with rare but equal temper, did the same. We crashed and bashed, a memory of our touchstone joyride long ago. We slowed to crash and crash again, oblivious to all the other cars, which ducked and spun in vain attempt to miss our little show. The flagman, not amused, threw go-home black our way, but we, in crimson fury, both ignored it. The flagman threw the red to stop all cars, but still we bashed and bantered, oblivious to the call.

Furious One-Eye waved me in with an acquiescent nod from Wylie; furious Spencer did the same for Wynn. Finally, Spencer, with an untoward glare, took a crowbar and walked to the center of the track, his arm raised high, daring both of us to pass him by. We didn't.

I'm not sure we could have. Steam rent the air from busted radiators. Splayed oil lines dripped telltale tracks around the course. I had two inflated tires left, of four; Wynn, but one.

The slapjack show thus ended.

Not quite.

Three nights later, it must have been, uncle One-Eye drew us close.

You kids are going to get the opportunity of a lifetime, he said. I don't know whether it'll come next year or five years from now, but it will come, and you'd best be ready when it does.

He then explained the presence of the dapper stranger in our midst, one whom I had noted briefly, nothing more.

His name is Jean-Pierre Andriotti, One-Eye said. He's a Dorsen honcho and he's scouting for his Circuit cars. He's looking for drivers with a pretty face who don't have police records and can keep a race car down between the hedges. He's heard of you and he's watching, taking notes.

Hey, no problem, I said.

It will always be a problem if you pull what you pulled last Saturday night.

Why are you looking at me? I didn't run into a damned telephone pole.

I know, said Wynn. You kept running into me.

If you'd been down where you belonged, I wouldn't have touched you, I said.

If you had been willing to admit I was whipping your ass, even with a sickly engine, said Wynn, you'd have backed off and parked your pile of shit. Sorry, One-Eye, but your donkey chauffeur here covered as much ground from top to bottom of the track as he did going around it.

The track is mine. I glared. Any part of it you want you'll have to come and get.

You arrogant prick, said Wynn. You are losing your hold on reality, and you are too much like your old man for me to even consider talking to you. As for you, One-Eye, I don't know what in hell you're up to, but I want no part of it. Sometime, if you dare, I'd like to know why you went back to the Mavis operation. I've thought it through from every angle. It doesn't calculate.

Now One-Eye's hackles flew, to bring distemper to a trio.

Listen up, the both of you, he said. Number one, what I do with my life is my business, none of yours. Number two, what you do with your lives is ultimately none of my concern—off the race track. But until you demonstrate to me you've found the handle and are hanging on secure, I'll busy myself in every way I can with what you do *on* the race track, like it or not. And that's the end of that.

He left. Wynn pouted. I sulked, withdrawn into an inner Mavis turmoil that was fast becoming home.

CHAPTER
21

I broke my maiden, long at last, at Ashley Oaks, a dry-slick quarter-miler, ten days exactly after One-Eye's lecture. I should have felt a joy at this pronouncement of my progress, but the victory, strangely, held no lasting charm, for the winning was less a credit to my skill than a result of other failures. The race was fifty laps, a dash. I worked my way to fifth and held, unable to mount a further charge. A spin, and I was fourth. Someone's sickly engine popped and I took third; a flattened tire, second; a broken tie rod, first. I looked around to see if others still pursued, and then the flagman sauntered to the center of the track and gave his checkered flag a desultory wave—and that was that. The next time by, I stopped, obtained the checkers, and held it high one final time around the track.

Andriotti sauntered by to offer polished kudos, sauntered off.

Why such joyless joy? The win, I knew, would come in time. Thus, when it did, it carried no surprise. And further, there was no one there with whom to share the moment. No fleshy Betsy to offer victory dalliance, no smiling One-Eye to give a proud and fond embrace. He had stayed behind to dream up speed tricks at his workbench. Not even Wynn, who'd called the season quits the week before, was there to offer me a reason for the victor's gloat. Only Wylie saw the moment, he who often traveled with me to gas my car, the only green-flag service necessary at a race date such as this.

Nice run, he said, declining further demonstration.

Thanks, I mustered.

We loaded up my car, which we in mutuality had burdened with the name of *Thunder III*, though it bore but faint resemblance to its whiskey-transport predecessors. We drove to our motel, a bleak and run-down wood-constructed place. Bugs and moths smashed and swatted up against the office window, seeking orbit round the pale yellow light inside. Exhausted, we took our key and stumbled to our room.

A further dullness there: two sunken beds with pancake mattresses that promised anxious, aching sleep; a basin and a shower stall; no more. Wylie carefully unlaced his lucky boots, polished them wet-rag clean, and placed them standing, gleaming, in a corner. He shed his oil-stained work shirt and his dusty trousers and set about the task of disassembling his brace. He'd fought the brace, proud crippled warrior, but without it he could barely stand, a wobbling totem. He'd tried a cane, a singular shillelagh Uncle Julian had brought one day, a peaceful offertory declined with vengeance, and then he'd briefly flirted with a walker, would have none of that.

It's for an old folks' home, he said.

The brace thus fashioned began with leather wrapped around his portside thigh. Two stainless steel rods extended past his calf, declined in size by atrophy, and fastened to a footplate beneath his ankle. This worked just fine in time, though occasionally he'd forget the piece—the tricky use of it as well—and stumble, burning daggers at his fate. When sitting, he could loosen up a pivot screw to downward fold his leg; when standing, walking, he'd simply lock it up again and trundle onward like a pegleg man. In time, and with his harsh determination, he grew quite agile in its use.

Whenever I saw him naked and exposed, such as now, my heart and brain churned mixed. He was an isolated man, the creature of his own convictions, the isolation first imposed by him and him alone, and then by others as they realized the keen futility of discourse. The way he chose forbade discussion of the whys of it, to such extent that I, his closest, never tried, though many times the questions ambled to my lips, there to die unasked.

The one I dared not ask the most, so central to the core of things it was, concerned, of course, his liaison with tawny Annalise. True to old predictions, their lusty meetings tapered quickly from the first engagement, though rumors flew that on occasion, right up to his accident, they would seek a place and find it. Why did he—how could he keep on doing—knowing full the myriad layers of his cruel betrayal? Did tawny Annalise possess a secret charm, a hidden way to soothe his hidden torment? If so, such charm, such methodology—save for her pouty beauty—she hid from nearly all the rest.

Wylie did not ever flaunt his tawny conquest—if, in fact, he was the conqueror and not the tawny one herself—

or ever indicate one way or another whether her charm and soothing had effect. The secret stayed within their nest, there to grow and fester, and with the Wylie crash, to die, no mention of it ever made before or after.

Such confusion in my heart and mind; such shy, intimidated inability to pursue the matter with its primal agent.

Wylie's withered leg was fair reminder of his unkind slashes. Yet, I declined—or so I hoped—to deny him understanding or benefit of doubt. I simply didn't know, and knew I lacked the highroad courage to pursue.

And there was still another crossing thought that gave me reconsideration's pause. I was a Wylie, after all, his seed and progeny. If in him dwelt a devil's cussed curse, then in me, too?

I cannot say our bullring travels brought me closer to him, or nearer to the understanding that I sought; I cannot say that. Our talk was racing talk: the twitching of the chassis, the tweaking of the engine, the selection of the gears and springs, the tires, caster, camber, toe-in, toe-out, the finding of the racing groove, the measuring of the opposition, the way to turn a corner, read a race track, worry rivals to submission unsuspecting. Wylie knew me well in such a talk; I knew him not at all.

So it was this night of broken maiden, Ashley Oaks. Wylie, naked, glimped into the shower and cleansed his body of its race-track dirt and grime. I did likewise, lingering long beneath the warm and purifying torrent, thinking sugar thoughts of Fiery Tongue and other places, similar; of tawny Annalise and fiery Wylie in their desperate embracing, smiled at that for all its painful repercussions; of One-Eye's close-held pain at *his* tawny-fiery imaginations;

of Miss Ma's sternly gentle loyal patience; of Annalise herself, now turned to Wynn for what was there for her to find. What was going on here?

I grabbed a towel and rubbed myself to pinkish glowing, found my pancake mattress and the sinking springs, and sank to sleep.

. . .

Aaaiiyaaugh . . . huh . . . huh . . . whoo.

A bone-chilled scream tore through the dank and suffocating air. And then another, and a third. I woke from sleep with startled suddenness, sought hard to gain my bearings and a sense of where I was, and why. I jogged into an anxious focus as the strangeness of the tawdry room came clear, and waited.

Aaaiiyaaugh . . . huh . . . huh . . . whoo.

Wylie! I sprang from concave achiness and fumbled for the bedside lamp. Wylie sat bolt upright, stunned and hollow-eyed, his hard and mottled body bathed in sweat, still lost, for sure, in fearsome, awful reverie.

Wylie! I shouted. Wylie! Wake up. You've had a dream. Wake up.

Huh . . . what?

He came around and looked beyond me, the fear entrenched, and settled slowly to the comfort of his waking, though stunned he stayed for several moments as I waited.

Huh . . . damn, he said. Goddamn. Andrew, in the bottom of my bag you'll find a pint. Pour me one. Be quick.

I found two dusty glasses at the basin and did as he instructed, one for him and one for me—why not? He threw the tumbler's cinnamon liquid down without a hint of whiskey ceremony and offered up the empty for a refill. I obliged and sipped my own.

You scared me nearly to the seventh heaven, I said. Did you flip a race car? Have a nightmare fall? Or what?

And thus my flippant introduction to Wylie's ancient torment:

It's always the same dream, said Wylie. The same fucking dream. I sometimes think I'm done with it. But once and twice a year, when I sleep alone in strange and far-off places on the bullring circuit, it comes back to haunt me in a terrifying way. I never had it over there, where it made sense to have it; never once did I have it over there. I was always so tired, so deathly, deadly tired. It wasn't just a day of waiting, and watching others writhe in fatal agony and die, but days and nights and other days, such long accumulation of the terror of the wait that my imagination's bonds were stretched to breaking, and beyond. I was so tired—we all were—I did not care to cling to life. Such tiredness denied me dreams. But nobody gave up. Some of us were loose-boweled scared—the chickenshits, we joked—but nobody gave up. You couldn't. But I was so tired that death in all its comfort became a thing to beg for, seek, embrace. I dreamed the dream the first time on the troopship coming back, when I was safe, no worse for wear than shrapnel-laden nicks and scratches, superficial, mostly, and it was safe to dream again. The dream's so real—colors, sounds, and smells, the works—now as then, that I no longer mark the difference of the truth of war and fantasy. That much has been denied me, now, and for twenty years and more has burned a fire in my brain and shaped my soul forever. Sometimes they'd meet us at the beaches, coral black and oiled with blood, and inch by inch—such tiny measurement—we'd gain a hold, and pause to breathe and view the bleakness all around us, and inchward move again. But other times they'd yield the beachhead free and clear, and that was worse. They sucked us in and let us march unimpeded and wary, twitching all the while, the knowledge known that they were out there, somewhere, waiting for a battle of their choosing, not of ours. They moved into their caves, limestone gray and bleak, and waited, a tunnel city doomed before the battle even started. That was what I never understood. The end result was preordained, inevitable, and we and they both knew it. Yet we took no prisoners, nor they. Not one on either side. They sucked us in and dared us to come after them. I dared. With a flamethrower. That was my job at the caves—to burn them out. First we shelled the caves, massive barrages that lasted for hours, filled the air with piercing, screaming projectiles that blasted against the pockmarked limestone walls. *Surrender, you bastards*. No damage, no result, no response. Then we moved closer, under deadly fire, and laced the caves with brutal deadly fire of our own from machine guns and automatic rifles. *Surrender*. With grappling hooks a squad scaled the walls to get above the caves and sling grenade packages into the caves. We could hear their screams of terror, now. *Surrender, surrender*. Then I'd strap the pack upon my back, a gasoline can is what it was, and move forward under cover from the small-arms fire of my squad, and stand before the cave. *Surrender, surrender, you sons of bitches*, I shouted, waited, heard nothing. I turned a handle to ignite my weapon, and out shot a tail of flame thirty feet and more, and shouting, screaming, pleading all the while, I pointed the nozzle at the mouth of the cave and waited to hear the awful screaming; watched with horror as one or two, human torches, fled the cave for the sanctuary of an enfilade to end their agony. Cave by cave I did this, and sometimes pillbox by pillbox: always the same beginning, always the same benumbing end. Cave by cave, and island by island, and month by month, no calendar sufficient to record such agony, theirs and mine. When that was done, the mop-up followed. I, with others from my squad, when the heat died low, found the entrance to the cave or pillbox, case by case, and cautiously, with rifles raised, checked the thoroughness of what I'd done. I was thorough. Huddled in a corner were the stinking, smelling corpses, smoldering still; huddled with their arms wrapped round each other as though such meager comfort could afford protection against their fiery end. I looked hard at them for sign of life—unlikely—and with a mounting horror looked harder still, for one of them was me.

Here Wylie paused to offer up his glass for a refill, then fumbled at the bedside table for a match and lit a cigarette, inhaled deep to let the sweet smoke fill his lungs, pursed his lips to exhale in a tiny, vigorous stream.

And now the dream goes topsy-turvy, flashback twisted, Wylie said. Now I'm in the cave, alone. My cave is dank and dark and closes in. Cobwebs build in the corners, and from the glistening ceiling there's water dripping, drop by drop. The beachhead is across the way, and in the intervening field, blasted to rocky stubble by all that's gone before, they come, hundreds of them, thousands, all with flamethrowers strapped upon their backs. I do not know whose army this might be, theirs or ours or still another, but they sure as hell know who I am. *Surrender, Wylie*, they shout. *Surrender, you bastard.* And still they march, these hundreds, thousands, toward my cave and me alone. I want to surrender, but I cannot. I am desperate to surrender, but I cannot move, and I cannot make my voice work. *I give up*, I shout. *I'm coming out.* But no sound emerges from my throat, and their advance continues, like

197

a rolling wave. *Surrender, Wylie.* But I cannot. Their movement over the rubbled field is slow and grim. Persistent. More troops are landing on the beach to swell their ranks. I hear the tromping of their boots. I hear their shouts. Why can't they hear mine? Closer and closer they move, until they stand, all thousands of them, in a semicircle at the entrance to my cave. They can see me clearly, clearly see that I'm but one against their hordes and wish to lay down arms. But I cannot surrender. Then, one by one, they turn the handles of their flamethrowers and point the nozzles to the sky. The sky is filled with crimson loathing, a fire cloud that stretches from horizon to horizon. And then the nozzles lower. One designated man steps forward by a step or two and kneels. I feel the searing heat warm the limestone contours of my cave. I watch in horror as the flames from this one nozzle march lower down the rock above my cave. I see the flames lap at the entrance, know that I am soon to be consumed. I feel the searing heat and see the nozzle pointed directly at my face. And then I scream the scream you heard.

Wylie paused once again, diminished even by the telling of his tale.

I dream a bunch, said Wylie. Lots of dreams, good dreams, dynamite 3-D Technicolor dreams. But all these other dreams I know I'm dreaming, and I just sort of sit back and watch me dream the dream, if you know what I mean. But this one's a different dream. This one's made the leap from dream to memory.

I nodded, was familiar with that sort myself.

I wanted to give up, Andrew. I wanted to quit over there. But nobody gave up, nobody quit—on either side. I was always so tired, not for a day or a week or an island, but for months, for all the years I was there. And I wanted to give up but could not. If you gave up, you were dead. If you didn't give up, you were still dead. What's the point?

A silence loomed between us. Words from me were not what Wylie wanted. He lay abed and lighted up another cigarette from the butt end of the first.

Catch the light, Andrew. I'll be okay now, till the next time. Get your sleep with what's left of the night. We've got a long tow tomorrow, from here to home.

CHAPTER
22

Spencer Tatum didn't retire, not exactly. He raced some still, but only at Four Corners, and only when the mood struck home, which wasn't often. With Wylie on the sidelines, he seemed to lack the goad for further effort.

What's the point in my running? Spencer asked. With Wylie gone, it's not the same. He was unique. I don't mean to talk of him like he's passed on, though as far as I'm concerned, he has—the racing part of him. I've had my fun, and I truly don't believe that I'd have done as much as what I did if I hadn't had a race-track crossing with him. There's not a total logic to a thought like that, but it's true, I swear. Besides, my first thrill was always working on the race cars and not the driving of them. I had fun running when I ran; have more fun now while working on Wynn's cars. God knows, he keeps me plenty occupied.

But still, he never did a formal hang-it-up.

A smart move on his part, said One-Eye. Race-car drivers don't retire, if they're savvy, and our Spencer's surely that. The problem with retirement for a race-car jockey is the unretiring later on. A driver drives a car near every day—though not a race car—and soon enough his reasons for retirement start to blur and fade. With the passage of a little time, a driver soon forgets the self-protecting touch of fear that cooled him through his race-track crises. He forgets that bones don't heal as quickly as once before. His fire for competition doesn't burn as brightly, and thus, his concentration cannot hold to see him through the ding-dong maze. And he forgets, and he straps up again, to try the comeback, and the first you know he's cut the line too fine and backed into a wall and wrecked a car. The lucky ones. But if you don't retire, the temptation's less by far. How can you come back to what you've never left?

So Wylie, who might have raced with special rigging had not the fight been drawn from him by his vicious crunch, and Spencer, who in the selfsame incident had lost his rival and his touchstone goad, declined, and left the further driving to their youngish, coltish heirs.

But they could bench-race, talk and jabber, with the old enthusiasm still intact. One-Eye saw the truth of this firsthand one night this cold December past, a windswept month that shriveled souls and gave the whiskey trade a boost. I left town, depressed myself, and according to my One-Eye missed an evening rare.

One-Eye and Wylie played with *Thunder III* to get it ready for the coming season. Though Wylie still lacked a fundamental understanding of a race car, beyond his well-honed instinct for what would and wouldn't work, the two of them were near a perfect blend. Stubborn Wylie, yes, not dumb.

On this keen night they left the shop at ten o'clock,

the closing hour of Miss Dee's, the place they sought. They parked at the bus terminal by the side of the restaurant, One-Eye driving; Wylie, as usual, refusing all help.

Damn, he said, twisting his limp leg out of One-Eye's car and reaching down to lock the brace in ambulatory setting. Damn and damn again. Wish the doctors had gone ahead and taken the damn useless thing off right there in the hospital. Would have saved me no end of trouble. Peg-leg Mavis. Would have gone with what the town thinks of me anyway. Don't you think, One-Eye?

The drizzle, fiercely cold, was powered by a bluster wind that blew in dead-eye from the northern mountains. One-Eye shivered in a fleece-lined flight jacket. Wylie wore a shirt, no more, yet beads of sweat popped on his forehead and upper lip from the exertion of his walk, though short.

Damn, he muttered when he reached the door. That's what we'll do, One-Eye, you and me. I'll have a peg leg fashioned and you an eye patch, and Andrew—what'll we get Andrew? A parrot? That's it—a parrot. It could ride with Andrew rollbar-perched inside the car. Damn, One-Eye, we'd be the meanest, cussingest team in the history of the bullrings: the Pirates of . . . the Pirates of *Pity*.

Wylie was loose in a way that One-Eye'd rarely seen before, having a grand exuberant time. They got to the door just as Miss Dee came to lock it. But she quickly yielded to Wylie's plea.

We are the Pirates of Pity, he bellowed to her puzzled face. And we demand our supper, right and true.

Hush up, Wylie, One-Eye, she said. There's only Spencer here anyhow. I haven't hardly fired up the stove tonight. The weather.

Do so now, my lady, awkward Wylie bowed. And

please ask Mr. Tatum to join our merry band—is two enough for a band, One-Eye?—if he has no other obligation.

Lightly touching One-Eye's arm, Wylie swept the floor with an imaginary feather hat, a gesture no doubt bought from Errol Flynn.

One-Eye saw a secret look of glee in Wylie's dark and sweat-lined face. He exchanged a silent shrug with much bemused Miss Dee.

With practiced solemnity of her own, in keeping with the evening's building spirit, Miss Dee asked Mister Tatum if he would care to join Mister Mavis and Mister Rivers at their table. Spencer paused, a hesitation not worth noting save that he and Wynn still stood accused, at least by Wylie, of the gas-tank sabotage—and none save Wylie, One-Eye, and I was even privy to the fact of treachery.

Be delighted, Spencer said.

Miss Dee picked up Spencer's silverware, brought it and him to Wylie and One-Eye's table. The trio ordered, by telling Miss Dee the desired thickness of their cut and its doneness, and the number of tamales.

I think I'll have a drink, said Wylie, puffed and full. Would any care to join?

With careful ceremony, Wylie set upon the table a hefty pint of Heyward's finest, dollars versus doughnuts the source was Waylon Kelley's still. One-Eye nodded acquiescence; Spencer proffered thanks, but opted for a beer. Spencer's beer be damned, Wylie lined up three water glasses on the vinyl, checkered tablecloth and poured an inch in each.

I propose a toast, he said.

The others of the trio nodded, raised their glasses.

To the best two mechanics in the history of racing: One-Eye Rivers and Spencer Tatum.

All cheered, clinked glasses, and quaffed the moon-shine straight. The 'shine singed throats and made its hasty passage to their unsuspecting stomachs.

If I am ever executed, Spencer blinked, the death jolt won't compare to but a single shot of Waylon's whiskey.

And I, a toast, said One-Eye, quick to speak before his tongue turned leaden.

Wylie took his cue, reloaded.

To Wylie Mavis and Spencer Tatum, my one-eyed genius said. The two best race-car drivers in the history of Stokes County.

Again, the trio nodded, clinked, and swallowed. One-Eye said this second shot was like he'd cut his throat while shaving—from the inside out. He looked at Wylie; Wylie stared brilliantly at Spencer, the beer drinker, already flushed, perspiring.

Hear, hear, said Wylie, pouring fuel once again.

To Andrew Mavis and to my son, Wynn, wandering Spencer said. May our sons live long and healthy, wealthy lives, unburdened by the sins and failings of their fathers.

One-Eye squinted, quickly cadged a glance at Wylie, and looked the other way to Spencer. They were locked in combat, neither blinking, neither blanching. They raised their glasses yet again, threw caution to the wind, and swallowed hard. This time, was the later One-Eye memory, he felt nothing in his throat at all.

Miss Dee brought tamales, then the steaks—or rather, steak. For it was but one piece of meat and must have weighed five pounds, the size, in truth, of a race-car wheel. Miss Dee sliced once to show its doneness. Clear juices flowed from this one cut to show the inside brilliant pink, a perfect medium-rare. She took away the serving platter, came back a moment later with the steak divided into equal thirds. Each lapped over the edges of its plate, hot flecks of grease still bubbling from its fat-lined rim.

This, said One-Eye, is as close to heaven as I'll ever get, I know.

Without a further word, Wylie swept his hand through his wild black hair and began. Spencer wiped his flushed full face, grasped blindly for his beer, and knocked it to the floor. One-Eye felt the fire in his stomach and heard Spencer and Wylie begin to roar as though from far away.

Iced tea, Miss Dee; iced tea, Miss Dee.

One-Eye joined the distant chorus, but not with any voice he'd call his own. And then for the next thirty minutes he did not speak a single word. Not one.

Wylie, I'm sorry you're not running anymore, said Spencer. Truly, I am. I've never had the chance to tell you properly before, and I mean it. You may not believe the truth of what I say, but it's not half as much fun without you.

Wylie was taken aback, but only for a moment.

We had some times, you and me, he said. We did. I appreciate what you're saying.

They raised their glasses high in strangely fond salute.

You know what I'm not going to miss, though, said Wylie, are these new Circuit speedways springing up all over.

You worried about the speeds? asked Spencer, in serious contemplation of his disappearing steak. The pole at bigger tracks is going for one hundred and seventy-five miles an hour, and more. So I read. You run much faster than that, your brain can't keep up. Whatever happens is over before you've got the time to realize it's happening.

Naaw, said Wylie. The speed itself wouldn't bother

me none, any more than it would the kids. You cautious types might find it preying on your mind, though. You make a mistake at that speed, and a guy's going to do more than just ding his car. But the speed wouldn't bother me. Get used to that. Hell, Spence, they had cars in Germany before the war that'd do two hundred miles an hour on the straightaway, but so what? They sure couldn't turn a corner that fast. What I'd miss is that you can't *drive* at those speeds. You can't *race*. All you are is a passenger, holding on. The Circuit racing is passing from the drivers to the damn mechanics. How much passing you think there is—door-knocking passing—at a hundred and fifty, a hundred and sixty miles an hour? You sure can't do any fender-banging at those speeds.

That's the part you liked best, wasn't it, Wylie? Spencer said. It wasn't a good pass if you didn't leave some of your paint on the other guy's car.

Spencer was smiling, but for how long, One-Eye couldn't say.

If there's no hole, you got to make one. There isn't anybody going to make one for you.

You'd be surprised, waiting a lap or two, how many holes open up. There are lots of ways to worry a guy without putting him in the damn fence.

You wait long enough and pretty soon the white flag's out, and then the checkers, and then the other guy's up there taking home the check and kissing the doll-babies, Wylie retorted, having brought his eating to a sturdy halt. That's what I never have figured out about you. You were good, Spencer, but you only won what the other guys gave you. You hardly ever won a race on your own. You never worked to *create* the checkers. You just waited around. I heard one guy—it was Bennie Mantz from down near

Terminus—say that being passed by Spencer Tatum was like a kiss from his sister: sweet and uneventful.

I take that as a compliment. Wonder what old Bennie said getting passed by you was like. Like getting blown off a mountaintop in dead of winter?

You got to let them know you're there, Wylie said again. Now, that boy of yours, I hope he gets himself some brains. He's got plenty of guts and plenty of talent, insofar as I can see. But you've got to be smart, too. Talent won't take you all the way.

Well, that started it. Waylon Kelley's finest was the fuel, and any mention of Wynn or me the spark. Wylie's taking out after Wynn, no matter how accurate the observation, aroused in Spencer a succinct verbal demonstration:

You're full of shit.

Spencer's eyes turned big and round and appeared to move closer to his nose. His mouth likewise drew into a circle, into which he stuffed half a cold tamale and washed it down with one shot each of 'shine and sugar tea.

I'll put Wynn against Andrew anytime and anywhere, in matched cars—we'll let One-Eye build them both—and we'll see who's got the brains and who doesn't. You think smart is tearing a race car all to hell—two race cars—just because Andrew's pissed off at the world? What Andrew started last fall was the kind of shit'll get you killed. That showed to me a lack of brains and character, both. What are you doing with that boy of yours? Life isn't made up of quarter-mile bullrings. Not for them. Not for long. He'll only try that crap once on a Circuit track and they'll pry him out of the car and bring him home in a plastic bag. Andrew's got an awesome anger, Wylie—can't imagine where he got it. I just hope he doesn't take anybody with him.

He isn't going anywhere, said Wylie, some subdued. It took two to make that little Donnybrook Fair.

Wynn isn't going to back off.

He'd best learn to move aside, the how of which he could learn from his old man.

The only passing to be done will be when Wynn starts lapping the field, Spencer said. Wynn's got more talent in his left foot than Andrew's got in his whole damned body.

And his talent's snuggled up right next to his brain, because that's where his brain is, too—in his left foot.

Wylie reached down and pulled up his own left foot in demonstration. He let it fall back to the floor with a dull loud thud.

We'll see on the big tracks who's got what, said Spencer. They'll both be there someday. Wynn will. Andrew will probably still be bouncing off of cars and bullring things.

A sullen pause descended.

To Wynn, concluded Spencer.

He raised his glass and quaffed, only mildly disappointed to find it empty.

To Andrew, toasted Wylie, filling his own glass and gleefully hiding the bottle from Spencer's shaky, lurching grasp.

Jesus Christ, burped One-Eye, breaking silence. Goddamn grown men making fools.

Carefully, he pried the bottle from Wylie's reluctant grasp. He grabbed three clean glasses from an adjoining table and meticulously arranged them at the corners of an almost equilateral triangle, the geometry of which, he vaguely recalled, made him proud. He poured. He stood. He toasted:

To the future. To the sons of giants.

Wylie and Spencer mulled that one over for a guarded time, found nothing there unsavory. They, too, stood and toasted sons of giants.

The tension splattered. One-Eye felt so happy with his successful peacemongering that he could not refrain from further comment.

Now that that's over, he said, let me ask you pair of towering giants about a bunch of things that have gone on between you two, beginning with that ruckus back in '56, I think it was. I've always been cur—

He got no further. Wylie grabbed him by the wrists, no easy task, and thrust him back into his chair. In a wild rage, Wylie rose from the table and tried to walk to the door. But he had forgotten to lock his brace and fell a-tumbling to the floor, flailing for support on his downward passage. He grabbed the checkered tablecloth. It and all upon it came tumbling down beside him in a crashing clatter. Wylie lay there, stunned, enraged, not hurt. Spencer and One-Eye rushed to his side. He refused their help. He sat up, grabbed a chair, and stood up, still declining to lock his brace. He held the chair from behind and used it as a walker. *Clump* went the chair as Wylie slammed it down, then hopped on his right foot, the left dragging fitfully behind. *Clump*, hop, drag; *clump*, hop, drag; *clump*, hop, drag.

One-Eye and Spencer watched in silent fascination as Wylie made his way across the floor. Miss Dee held the door open, and Wylie clumped, hopped, and dragged his way past her without so much as a nod.

He worked his way in the raw night air down the sidewalk to One-Eye's car. Before he sat down, he took the chair and leaned against the car and threw the chair in the direction of One-Eye and Spencer.

He's a poor excuse, muttered Spencer. A damned poor excuse.

One-Eye simply stared, sad and shaken.

CHAPTER
23

I'm flying.

They've strapped me to a sled beneath the beating rotors, a tethered, rope-wrapped wreckage. One-Eye lingers, shouts a final word, its meaning lost beneath the windy din. The rotors up their beat. I'm facing to the rear, so that when the delicate lift begins, the tail's rising sends a gentle flush of blood into my brain, already crimson-stained. We rise, slowly, slowly, to a clearance height, and with a headstrong rush I'm off. The sun is warm. On my face I feel a cooling breeze from the rotors' flaccid flapping as we achieve a sailing altitude. The rotors ease their beating now, and settle to a cruising pitch. The sound once again diminishes. The soft declension brings a welcome peace.

Often, when I lie awake at night, alone, and stare beyond the trees, beyond the rising moon and velvet, diamond-studded sky, disinclined to sleep, I hear a guttural roar from the direction of the Speedway. Some kid from town—or maybe not from town—has found the whorish bullring, broken up the chain, and taken to the rudely rutted track for thrills and chills.

He's out there by himself, in a hot rod of his own, his headlights flashing on the red-clay dirt ahead, a girl, perhaps, reclining on his shoulder. I love the sound, as well as the scene imagined. It brings a teary trembling, always, a reminder of all I've lost and failed to gain.

I listen carefully, try to judge the skill and courage of this other, younger self. The laps go on, the engine's distant rumbling revealing all I need to know. Some are slow; others smooth. Most are smooth and slow. Now and then—the ones I most appreciate—there's a mighty roar as one with stones for brains attempts to test the racer's edge.

I slip each trial into known, familiar categories: this one, slow and smooth, is Uncle Julian; that one, fast, erratic, is bloodhound Wynn; still another, rumbling evenly, must be a Spencer. Those are all the categories that I have. For Wylie and for me there're none. No duplicates emerge from such an evening's thunder play, no matter how hard I listen for a fit. There are no others like us, him and me.

We've taken off into the wind, toward three and four, and climbed above the guard rail, there to pivot. I feel the slowing, sense the hanging in the air as the helicopter swings and turns, and now heads back across the infield.

I wish that I could see the scene below, the one of my creation, but all is still a crimson darkness. What would I see? A gnarled guard rail in number four, no doubt; a scar across the track from where the undercarriage of my shark-like car dug in; the vivisectioned car itself in scattered bits and pieces here and there; a knot of people looking up. Or would they look?

The chopper with its damaged goods descends, a snow-

212

ball rolling down an airy hill. We reach the point, I know, where directly down beneath us lies the dogwood grove, full-bloomed, the flowers terminally resplendent in their short season of fragile beauty.

I wish to linger here. But no, I dream a dream I've often dreamed before.

I am in a race car on a race track. The track is red-clay dirt, but of huge and singular dimensions. A towering grandstand on the front straight holds, by estimation, a hundred thousand screaming, cheering fans. As I pass by, running flat-out wide within bare inches of their noses, I look for soothing faces, but cannot find a single one. Then I look elsewhere, atop the sturdy, stubby wooden posts to which is strung the guard rail. Each post has on it one black bird, but as I take a second look, these raven birds, by separate turns, transmogrify, and change to all the people I've ever known. There's Annalise, and Betsy, and One-Eye, and Uncle Julian, and Miss Ma; Heyward, Dozier, Billy Winslow, Miss Dee, Preacher Rollins, each in turn. Even the Colonel's taken wing. As I pass them by, each one, they flutter giant wings and gain a newer perch upon my race car.

Up ahead, the race track. I am running solid fourth. Before me, there's an old, familiar trio. Left to right, dueling three abreast and in their duel pulling me behind, are Wylie in his whiskey car, Rex Harding in his Indy car of darkness black, and Dink MacIntosh in his airplane, a fact I do not see in any way irrational.

We hurtle down the front straight, I, picking up my aviary passengers as we go, and round the first turn, slide in and out the second, and fire down the back straight.

There is no third turn. At the point where such a turn

should be, there is no race track. There's not a drop-off, not a void. There's nothing there, and worse, there's even absence of a nothingness.

This is my dream, my nightmare. The members of the trio near that point, and one by one they disappear. I, too, approach the wall, but resist with all my might the others' fate. I jab the brake, but only pick up quiet speed. I flick the wheel to start a spin, but stay my present course. I open wide my mouth to bellow fiercely at this perversion, so unsought, but there's no sound.

I wake up pooled with sweat, having jarred as well the Mavis household, or, if elsewhere, my once and former sugar, Betsy.

Maybe I'm dreaming now. Maybe all I have to do to wake is scream a curdling scream and I'll be back to where I was. Which would be where?

No.

CHAPTER
24

And so at last to present April, a time in every year—so say the gentle thinkers—of hope and fond renewal after winter's bleak repression. The misty gloom of cold and rain-chilled nights yields at last to quiescent optimism of sun-spanked days. The earth blooms, and Heyward Scrivens orders up his sugar tea.

The poet argues otherwise, says April is the cruelest month, a time of fractured dreams and empty teacups rattling in the wasteland. Much depends on where one lives.

In Four Corners, there was much to choose from, either way.

In January, Jean-Pierre Andriotti had burst in town to formalize the black-box trial, Wynn's and mine, an encounter so surprising that it warped all other thinking from my mind. On tenth of March came news of Dink Mac-Intosh's ungainly aeroplane demise, a sad occasion, to be sure, but fringed with smiles in memory of that effervescent, clownish sport—and adding heavy weight, I can't deny, to the import of our test, bare weeks away.

The first race of the season, at Four Corners, was April 4. Nothing fancy, this one. The outlaw race for bullring whiskey cars and Circuit cars alike, a longtime start-up staple, had faded with the changing times as the monster asphalt Circuit speedways, as well as the special race cars thus required, slowly shouldered out the bullrings. The show would be two heats, a trophy dash, a consolation—if sufficient cars towed in, a question—and then a long and tiring two-hundred-lapper main. A shakedown race, it was, for cars and drivers, and especially for the track. To complicate the matter was a gush of torrent rain that fell for three days straight in prelude to the race. Heyward couldn't work the racing surface much at all, and gave instead his time to pumping dry the infield to avoid the bogging down of cars and rigs in sucking mud.

I rue the day I built this place, said Heyward on the racing eve.

He stood in waders in the center of the muckety-muck, glowering, as his electric pumps waged losing war against the onslaught, and who could blame him?

Though rain had stopped, the track was still a mess the morning of the race, and Heyward had a passing thought to cancel. But several drivers had towed in from distant points, and Heyward soon declined the notion. No spectators graced the infield, still a quagmire despite the pumps. Pools of standing water collected at the bottom of the turns, and all the way around the track the lowest lane—as well the pits—was sloppy. Still, the upper racing grooves were hard and firm—greasy-slick, not dry-slick, one could say —and a midday sun that strove with noble gallantry to ease the airy chill and break the stolid cover of the clouds gave hope the race could be accomplished with a minimum discomfort.

Wylie was excited, in his strange impassioned way, at the rising of another racing season, his second on the side-lines, my second at the wheel. As we entered to the pits, he and I and One-Eye, he did a ceremony he'd performed at every race he'd been to since his accident. The reaction of the racing folks to Wylie's crunching fall was mixed. On one hand this: What do you say—if driver or mechanic, makes no difference—to one who's been done in by circumstance that easily could befall yourself in turn? On the other: Guessing had it half the drivers there, deep down, would not have minded in the least had one of them been called to be the agent of his mishap.

Lock your brace, One-Eye said. Now don't forget.

Yaas, said Wylie. I reckon there's a bunch out there who'd like to see me fall flat on my face. Now isn't that the truth?

You just might be on the mark with that, I said.

We three got out of One-Eye's car. Wylie slipped the flatbed hitch, and I and One-Eye pushed the latest *Thunder III* to its appointed place in the middle of the pits.

Here goes, said Wylie.

This was fully thirty minutes before our practice would begin. The fans were slow to fill the grandstand, but the pits were full of busy crews and drivers. Wylie gimped the length of them, and back, giving all who wanted two clear shots at him. He walked ramrod straight the first time by, like an old and ghostly general reviewing parade-ground troops the last and final time. On his second passage, though, he met the eye of each and all who deigned to match his blazing nugget gaze. Heyward, so I noted, was much bemused by such a pandy show, but dared not indicate his humor. Of the others, many turned away, busy-work excused from such a haughty, heartless gesture. A few, namely Wynn and Spencer, went off their way to shake his hand.

Practice started, and with my second lap at speed, I saw there'd be a problem. I nestled in behind another car, just goofing, but when we twisted for the turn I suddenly was blinded. The sticky gluck from the other's spinning wheels had splashed my windshield to near opacity, and by several car lengths I backed off. Damn. I knew right there and then there'd be a lot of frantic windshield scraping come the race itself, by me and all the others.

At my pit stops, we decided, Wylie was the one to do the gassing, his usual task. One can only would be needed. The gassing was a tricky task. The waist-high canister, torpedo-shaped, was an awkward weight. To raise it high and mate the nozzle with the tank required skill and burly strength when done the proper way, with speed and firm finality. One-Eye's foremost job would be the windshield and the hosing down of *Thunder III* as much as pit-stop time permitted.

For so early in the season, on such a mucky sloppy track, the race was ding-dong all the way. Or so I gathered, watching all the cars fly by. I had my problems from the green flag onward, and once the lapping started, I lost all count of my position: of mine or Wynn's or anybody else's. Once and twice the feverish sun poked through the clouds and bathed the track in brief and gentle warmth. I looked to Wylie and to One-Eye each and every time I trundled past, all the while wishing I could join them on the sidelines. My engine purred, and *Thunder* handled like a dreamboat. But I was backing up and getting lapped and flailing away with less and less to show. A misery.

We had a number system for communication: 1 for gas; 2 for handling; 3 for tires; 4 for oil pressure; 5 for engine temperature. We used numbers, not the words, and changed the numbers every race to hide from others what our own concern might be.

So. One-Eye chalked the numbers when he realized my plight, and each time by, count five, I shook my head. The next time by the pits, he flashed a simple question mark: ?

I nodded stiffly, at the same time covered up my eyes. Straight ahead, I couldn't see at all, save for a tiny spot of clearing that I'd fashioned on my own by reaching out and wiping off the windshield. But this was not a trick to last forever, and the warming sun, though somewhat welcome, made the matter worse, on balance, by drying, caking what was there already.

We'd planned for me to pit two-thirds the distance. But on lap eighty-eight, the yellow flashed—for what, I, blinded, never knew—and half the fleet came storming in. I charged the pit road, steaming hard, and waved with vigor at the villain windshield. I hit the pits a bit *too* hard, saw One-Eye standing with his hands raised up to mark the spot where I was asked to stop, and slid a goodly, gooey ten feet more beyond, with the rear of *Thunder III* cocked well out into the middle of the pit road. It was an interesting job of angle parking, to be sure.

One-Eye gave me a dirty look and I returned the same, though there was little time for chatterbox recrimination. One-Eye grabbed a water hose and doused my clogged-up radiator, then turned the hose upon my windshield. At the other end of *Thunder III*, I watched through rearview mirrors as gimpy Wylie hobbled to my gas tank lugging with him his torpedo burden. He twisted hard the screw cap, tethered to the car by safety wire, and drove the gas-can nozzle home and poured.

I held my left foot on the depressed clutch, and heel-

and-toed my right foot on the brake and gas—all this to keep the car in place with engine racing. Straight ahead I stared, knowing that the race was lost but willing not to slack unless the car fell down on me. Whatever else, that much of Wylie had surely come my way.

What happened next is blurred, a fuzzy red-mud tapestry I wove together at a One-Eye sit-down reconstruction.

The gas-can nozzle stuck hard inside the tank. Wylie shouted. One-Eye dropped his hose and ran toward Wylie's post. From out the corner of my eye I saw the flagman signal one lap more, is all, before the green-flag restart. Anxious not to be a straggler, desperate not to lose another lap, I turned my head to seek a signal and thought I heard my One-Eye holler:

Go!

I popped the clutch and jammed the gas, twin actions that contrived to swing the cockeyed rear of *Thunder III* to the inside of the pit road in a spray of clammy mud. One-Eye—who'd said *No!* not *Go!*—leapt clear. Taken by surprise, Wylie once more yanked to free the gas can's neck from the gas tank's taut embrace. He succeeded well. But with the sudden flailing of the rear of *Thunder III*, he lost his balance and, with his left knee braced and locked, he sprawled head-first, still grasping at the gas can like a drunk holding to a lamppost.

Safe removed, One-Eye moved to verge of laughter at the pratfall sight, but heard instead the words of pit-road terror:

Car's loose!

Even as he heard the terror yell, he sensed an unnatural sound uptrack—not so much a sound as a sense of caterwaul disturbance: prickly air. With prickly instinct he flashed a rightward look and saw a car coming at him, at him and Wylie, at what seemed to be a hundred miles an hour, though in fact it could have been no more than twenty-five or thirty. Backwards.

He looked at it, at Wylie, back at it, and shouted:
Look out, Wylie!

The rest was frozen freeze-frame which I, no more than forty, fifty feet ahead, was rearview witness to as clearly as if I'd been standing there myself. The other car slid irrevocably toward Wylie, sprawled on the muddy track, his hard, tenacious arms clutching the torpedo gas can.

Wylie reacted well. There was no time to rise and run. With his braced and battered leg, he had no time to even crawl. He looked, then twisted himself in such a way that the gas can, still firmly in his grasp, was a shield between him and the runaway car. He curled up around the tank and waited.

The right-rear wheel of the backward-moving car hit the tank and lifted up and knocked Wylie's left shoulder loose from the tank; left him sprawled and helpless. A split second later the right-front tire rolled over the tank and then over Wylie's chest with a squish-thump sound.

Goddamn, said a voice behind One-Eye, a voice filled with reverence and awe.

Goddamn, said the voice. That fellow went and done killed himself.

One-Eye ran to Wylie—there wasn't far to run—and knelt, but there was no point. Wylie's face was engorged with blood and terror. His chest was soft. A thin trickle of blood ran from his mouth down to the corner of his chin. He didn't move.

The gas can lay nearby, slightly dented.

All this I saw.

The race was yellow-flagged again. I and the other drivers stayed on the track, slowly turning laps. With curiosity mingled with respect, several in the pits came over to see, kept their distance.

The car! One-Eye said he prayed that the death car was neither Wynn's nor Spencer's. That would have been too much. It wasn't. The driver was a kid from Terminus named Dexter Fales, a regular bullring driver of no particular distinction. He'd pitted strongly, just as I had, and had gotten clipped and turned around by another car. He sat in his car, head and hands resting on the steering wheel, made no move to get out.

The ambulance picked up Wylie's body and with no siren drove across the track and out the gate by turn one. It stopped by the grandstand, and Miss Ma and Uncle Julian slowly climbed in.

The yellow flag waved for twelve laps. One by one the cars pitted, just to check things out. There was nothing to lose. I stayed out on the track. Each time I drove by the pits, part of a grumbling line of cars in slow single file, One-Eye waved me in. I stared straight ahead, ignoring him. One-Eye went to the race steward and asked that I be black-flagged to force me in.

We were going to anyway, said the steward. His gas cap's not screwed on.

I ignored the black flag as well, waited for the restart. *Thunder III* was the first car in line behind the pace car. I jumped everybody on the restart. I came off four, hard, kept my steering wheel cocked, and powered down the front straight, nearly catching up the pace car. I stayed high up on the track, up where nobody had run all afternoon, my churning, driving wheels spraying the grandstand with mud.

I drove possessed, but by what I didn't know, and I drove not very well. I grabbed the attention of everbody. The other drivers gave me a long tether, kept their wary distance.

For five full laps I drove like this, high and wild, spraying clumps of mud while the black flag flew and the other drivers cowered. One-Eye gave up. He stood by our tool box and raised a foot up on the dented gas can.

The sixth time by, I depressed the clutch and kept my foot on the gas. The engine wound higher and tighter and sought its breaking point. A banshee wail. *Thunder III* slowed, coasting high on the outside of the track toward turn one, slowly, slower. I rested my head on the padded steering column and gripped the wheel mightily, my arms bent and locked at the elbows.

Slowly, slowly now, I drove, while the engine screamed its banshee scream. Slowly. I kissed the guard rail in turn one, my engine screaming for release.

I cut the ignition.

CHAPTER 25

That night the family gathered, at Brandy Logan's funeral parlor—gathered, actually, in the long and narrow living room of Brandy's house, for the death business was not a heavy call in Stokes County. Occasionally, Brandy had his schedule conflicts, but once or twice a year at most, no more.

Uncle Julian was there, nervous and distraught. Aunt Melvina was there. She had gone directly to the hospital, taken Miss Ma home, where both sang a wailing song, and at Miss Ma's insistence helped select the clothes for Wylie's laying out. They found an ancient suit, one in which I'd not seen Wylie twice. No dress shirt could be found. Brandy quick produced one of Wylie's size and fit, though I could only wonder at the prior service it had seen. From somewhere long ago Miss Ma fetched up a necktie, silken blue, with race-car patterns woven in its thread. So there we were. The parlor room was long and narrow, dark. Wylie's casket, open, occupied one end. Aunt and uncle occupied two chairs along one wall, and opposite, Miss Ma, glistening radiant in a tragic way. I, still dressed for racing, not yet cleansed of race-track sweat and grime, stood by the casket and met my Wylie's closed-eyed gaze at last. And so the family gathered, and one other.

One-Eye sat alone, slumped and nestled in a corner of a heavy couch at the opposite end of the room from the bier. There I walked to sit beside him, share a cigarette.

Explain, I said, my mind atwimble.

I've seen worse deaths at the race track, but none was closer, so One-Eye said. Death is part of racing, sure and true, but every time it happens it's the first one over once again. Strange to say, I feel no loss, not yet, though that will surely come, even as it did with Mae, my long-lost loving Mae. Death's the opposite of birth, and that's the thought that hit me first. I saw my baby Annalise, not yet named, within the minutes of Mae's deliverance. I saw her, touched her, kissed, caressed her—and felt nothing. Where was the grand passion I was supposed to feel for the fruition of my seed? Where? Well, the overwhelming loving came, but not for several days and even weeks. And all the waiting time I wondered: Where? And so it is with Wylie, his gossamer thread now slashed, this strange and passionate man with whom I cast my fortune, twice, despite an arm's-length worth of reasons not to. The loss will come, I'm sure, but not for several days. And you?

I walked back to the casket, no answer at my lips, and none from Wylie's. We sat in silence, all, and waited. Finally, weariness descended, and to Miss Ma I turned.

Go home, I said. There's nothing more to do.

Are you coming?

I'll be along. Don't worry. Aunt Melvina and Uncle Julian will be with you.

They left, and from the rear, our One-Eye made his

move to do the same. Without a word I motioned him to stay. The room was now so dark that I could barely make him out, his weary face half-lighted by a single table lamp. I moved behind the casket, lit another cigarette, and then began to speak. To One-Eye? To Wylie? I don't know. To me?

Dear friend, so I began with muffled hollow voice. Goodbye. Your passing is my loss and my salvation. You crippled me and others round you with your bitterness and hate. Yet you were the strongest man I've ever known, and by your death you pass that strength to me. The demon nightmares burned your soul, brought close the blood-red memories of a world in chaos and disorder, gave you license to live beyond the code. You never told us of your turmoil. Not Miss Ma, not uncle-brother Julian, not me but once— why then?—not we and others who cried out for your intimacy, but so silently and inward that you never heard our cries. I cannot forgive you, Wylie. I have some small and fragile understanding, like a dim and flickering light from deep within a stultifying cave. Forgive me that which is my legacy, never to forgive. And yet, no longer am I in your thrall. I saw you sprawl behind my car and take the blow of twin deliverance, yours and mine. I saw it all—the silent ambulance taking you away, and Miss Ma getting in beside you, and One-Eye's signals and the blackened flag. I saw it all, though I denied what certainly I knew. Such agitation built in me as I drove the yellow track, the engine of my *Thunder* sputtering at such slow speed. I built to such a tingling sweat such as I had only known in contemplation of *my* death and dying, a cold and terrifying sweat that threatened blindness and paralysis. I saw the green flag fly again—did I jump the start?—and drove with

fury to embrace the death that I had willed myself to
ignore. I drove possessed; possessed I was. And then, the
last time by, my engine screaming, I felt the demons leave
and knew that I was free. And so I do not grieve for me,
dear Wylie, for by your death you've given me release.
I grieve for thee, but with a heart as cold as stone. For I
cannot forgive.

I looked my final time at Wylie and kissed him gently
on the forehead, closed the casket.

From One-Eye's end I heard a muffled conversation.
Uncle Julian was back.

How's Miss Ma? asked One-Eye. And Melvina?

They're fine, said Julian. Miss Ma's fine. She's quiet,
stoic, strong. She wants Andrew.

I'll be home shortly, I said.

Julian was askew, agitated.

Don't leave just yet, he told me. We've something to
talk about.

Is everything okay? I asked.

Yes, yes, no, he stammered.

I'll be leaving, One-Eye said, and stood again to go.

Julian's shoulders slumped. His whole body sagged
into One-Eye's sofa.

Stay, One-Eye, he said.

I'll leave, said One-Eye. I'll let you talk with Andrew,
if that's what you came back to do.

No, said Julian, and then to me:

I killed your father.

It didn't register.

What do you mean? I finally said. You change your
name to Dexter Fales?

I put water in his gas tank, said Uncle Julian, hoarse

and flat. I didn't mean for Wylie to get hurt. I didn't even want a damn accident. All I wanted was for his engine to sputter and he'd have to park it and that would be the end of the winning streak.

It wasn't immediately clear what Julian was talking about. Wylie has a bad accident . . . is crippled . . . eighteen months later he stumbles in the pits and gets run over . . . What?

One-Eye caught the message first.

How'd you switch? he asked.

Aaw, One-Eye. It's so damned casual in the pits. Andrew asked me to fill a gas can and I did. Half of it with water. I didn't even know if it'd work.

Heyward put you up to this, I said, a declaration.

No. He didn't know about it. Nobody does.

I do, said One-Eye. And Andrew.

Julian was flabbergasted, looked to One-Eye, then to me, for explanation.

One-Eye gave it, saying that we knew the how, but not the why or who.

Heyward didn't know, Julian repeated. I was going to tell him after the race, if it worked. Heyward was furious with Wylie. Wylie was my brother and all, and I'm sorry as I can be he's dead . . .

You ought to be, snapped One-Eye.

. . . but he sure could piss off a lot of people in a lot of ways. Heyward thought Wylie greedy and arrogant. Couldn't understand why Wylie wouldn't stand down for a race or two. But Heyward wasn't involved. He didn't know.

Was Heyward into you? I asked. What did he have on you?

Nothing, Andrew.

228

Then why? asked One-Eye.

But there was obvious answer in the long, ongoing list of Wylie sibling slights and snubs, slights in front of family and of friends that were excessive for dark Julian's sins, if such they were.

I was quiet for a long time. Julian waited, for what, I don't know. A dressing down? A whambelly? Call Sheriff McCartle and lock him up?

Anybody else know what you're telling? I asked.

I'm telling you, Andrew. Who else is there to tell? —no offense, One-Eye. I wasn't trying to kill him, just to bring him down a notch to where the rest of us are.

Then here the tale stays, I said. Dexter Fales got loose in the pits and ran over a gas man who stumbled because his driver pulled away from the pits too soon. Here the story stays. There's no reason I can see to give it further audience. Agreed?

. . .

The weather gained a similar release as mine. On Tuesday, of interment day, huge waves of hot soft air rolled in, propelled by flusty gusting winds. False spring; a summer false. The sanctuary of the Baptist church was in dimension of a one-room country schoolhouse, and the mourners' list was short, to hardly anyone's surprise. Heyward came, and Dozier, and even Billy Winslow from the country store. Tawny Annalise and sugar Betsy added life to dead proceedings, their mourning clothes no match for their peacock fairies' beauty. One-Eye chose to stand at sanctuary's rear. Uncle Julian and Aunt Melvina took their places in the first row, left of center aisle. Spencer and his bloodhound Wynn, no longer on suspicion's hook, arrived separately and sat the same. Then Wylie's entrance came, and steps behind the rolling casket, dry-eyed calm

229

Miss Ma, and I, a gentle hand beneath her elbow. As we walked the center aisle, I caught the eye of Andriotti winking silently in my direction.

There was no sound save for Uncle Julian's muffled snuffling. There were no flowers, a declination of Miss Ma's, save for a singular wreath of yellow chrysanthemums with a single brilliant orchid in the upper-left quadrant. It sat at the foot of the casket, now closed.

The church was plain, austere, a fair description, too, of Preacher Rollins.

I don't remember much of this. My mind was elsewhere. There were hymns and chanted prayers. Preacher Rollins spoke of Wylie's good and decent works, altering for such occasion the few he knew about and making up the rest. He spoke of Wylie's love for family, and said he was a good and kindly man who wrestled serpents and in his own peculiar way found accommodation with the world in which he lived and the one to which his soul had recently departed. Will Rollins, so I understood, was less afflicted with the grand hypocrisy that like dust bolls follows men of cloth, and so he did not fabricate dead Wylie's worth beyond the minimums.

The service ended inside an hour. At its close, just as swirling winds were near their midday peak, I heard a sudden rustling in the seats behind me. Several men, race-car drivers all, walked purposely out of the church. Some were dressed in suits, others in khaki pants and work shirts. Andriotti, somewhat to my surprise, took his place among them. Once outside, this ruffian band—except, of course, for Jean-Pierre—formed a double rank on either side of the rude gravel path that led from the church door to the street. There were maybe twelve in all: Wynn and Spencer, Jean-Pierre, brave and solemn Dexter Fales, others.

Wylie's casket, now borne by six members of a Marine honor guard from Terminus, slowly and clumsily made its way up the aisle, with Miss Ma and me again behind. Up the narrow aisle it went, and through the great double doors, and down the steps to the gravel path. Slowly, slowly now, Wylie Mavis moved past the ranks of his peers, who stood at varying degrees of attention. I held Miss Ma back until the passage ended. What could be their thoughts? Jean-Pierre, who had suffered this ritual a score of times on several continents—one of his grand tales was about the overwhelming magnificence of a High Mass offered at the great cathedral at Chartres, for an obscure French driver who had killed himself at Le Mans in an act of unforgivable stupidity—and bloodhound Wynn stood accidentally side by side. Their faces had the same expression: solemn, awe-struck, and also pleading for some small mercy. What, I wondered, did mine show?

At the very end was Spencer Tatum, his bland round face a welt of quiet confusion. I could only imagine the years of memories coursing through him. As the casket passed him by, in a gesture so personal that I doubt it had a witness, save for me, he raised his right hand almost to the corner of his eye and held it there, a last salute to one who'd been his friend and rival, goad and touchstone, all these many years.

Brandy Logan escorted the members of the funeral party to their cars, Miss Ma and I to the first behind the hearse, Uncle Julian and Aunt Melvina to the second. Then Brandy handed out windshield stickers to the others of the motorized procession, though, given time of day and size of caravan, this hit me oddly. Brandy once had interned in the biggest funeral home in Terminus, and there, he said, they always used the stickers. Brandy thought they added class.

I saw Jean-Pierre climb in One-Eye's car, later heard from One-Eye of their shortened conversation on the cemetery drive.

Did you fly in from Detroit for this? One-Eye asked.

No, no, said Jean-Pierre. I was down in Ashley Oaks for the weekend, among other reasons to check the progress of the cars that Wynn and Andrew will test for us at Terminus. As I've said, I don't have to go out of my way for racing funerals. They happen to occur near where I happen to be. That's all.

They drove a distance, Andriotti pensive.

Someday, he said, you will have to tell me all about this Wylie Mavis. He was apparently not all that he seemed?

Nobody is, said One-Eye, though some would say he was quite a bit more than he seemed. He had his ghosts, his demons. He wasn't a bad man, Jean-Pierre. Some parts of this world overwhelmed him, is all.

These spirits, these demons—did Wylie pass them on to Andrew?

No, said One-Eye, lying. They were Wylie's alone. He wrestled them well, as Preacher Rollins said.

It was a touching irony I'd not before considered that the Stokes County Memorial Gardens, the place where Wylie's final rest would be, was in location directly adjacent to the Four Corners Speedway, one vacant lot, only, intervening between Heyward's first turn and the cemetery's first headstones. The cemetery was barren down below, but up a genteel slope there was a glen of loblolly pines, windswept, leaning to the leeward side. There was where we headed after disembarking from Brandy's shining, glistening limousines. We took our places by the casket; next to it the hole.

Will Rollins moved with admirable speed at this final

reassembling. We four of family sat, Uncle Julian still producing noises; the rest stood by in little clusters, threes and fours. The winds flapped the canopy and set the shrouds to whistling. The captain of the honor guard folded the American flag that had covered the casket and presented it to Miss Ma. With a sharp shake of her head, she declined. Flustered, momentarily, the young captain—he looked to be no more than one year, maybe two, my senior—turned toward Preacher Rollins.

Give it to me, I whispered.

This done, Will uttered nearly silent words from Scripture, then came to us to offer final comfort words. My ears turned dumb.

It was over.

As Miss Ma and I walked back down the hill to our limousine, I sensed the whoosh of release from those behind me, no longer mourners. They congregated in little groups, chatted amiably about anything, everything: the strange weather, racing stories, Wylie, of course, the news from Terminus and beyond. I wished to join them, caught a fragment of chitchat between dear Jean-Pierre and Wynn.

I hope this weather holds for two more weeks, said Jean-Pierre.

Your cars aren't mudders? Wynn asked to draw genial laughter.

Not on Terminus asphalt, they're not, said Jean-Pierre. Besides, in horse racing, a muddy track works to give advantage to the underdog. Fancy horses can't prance in mud. The same principle holds for your American football, I've observed. I want my cars to prance, as well as my drivers.

I'll prance, all right, said Wynn, his smile as buoyant as his optimism.

I'm glad to hear that, I heard Jean-Pierre say with easy

sincerity. I wouldn't expect anything else, from you or Andrew.

Miss Ma climbed into the back seat of the limousine. I prepared to shut the door. I turned in time to see Dexter Fales, shaken and red-faced, his frail frame balanced precariously in his distress, walk across the open space between the canopy and limousine and grasp Miss Ma's hands with his own.

I am so sorry, he whispered. I am so, so sorry. Forgive me, if you can.

There is nothing to forgive, said Miss Ma. Thank you, son, for all your strength, but there is nothing to forgive. I don't hold you to blame. Don't worry yourself more than you have already.

I made a mistake, said Dexter.

I suppose you did, said Miss Ma. But you're not the first to pit a car backward. And that wasn't the cause of what happened, anyway. Don't blame yourself, please.

Dexter looked at me. I nodded affirmation of Miss Ma's words. He walked down the hill and away from the cemetery.

Others from the hot and windy hill, seeing Dexter's courage, followed. One-Eye came and clasped, said nothing. Wynn and Spencer did the same, and Annalise, and Betsy, to whom this latest I raised an eyebrow, smiled.

Jean-Pierre was last. With practiced air, a just-right formal touch to keep his rank and distance clear, he gave condolence to me and then again to Miss Ma.

I did not know your husband well, Mrs. Mavis, he said. But I am sure he was an extraordinary man. I should have taken the time to know him better.

You might not have liked him as much if you had, Miss Ma said.

I looked for a twitch of a smile. There was none. She looked hard at Jean-Pierre.

Take care of my son, Mr. Andriotti, she said.

I will, Mrs. Mavis, though I hardly think—

Take care of him.

CHAPTER
26

The swayback town of Madison, on Highway 77
nearly at the halfway point between Four Corners and
Terminus, was in the main unfriendly territory, being in
the county south of us and thus beyond the influences of
Heyward and his brother-sheriff Dozier. Still, there was a
safe house there, of sorts, run by one all called Miz Abernathy. No one asked her first name; nor did she ever volunteer such.

A simple rooming house, it was, by all appearance:
wood-framed, painted white, two stories, a gabled roof. It
stood alone on the far southside of town, one block west-
ward from the highway on a cool and shaded street. It was
a magnificent rambling structure. The shuttered windows
—all were shuttered—were a gay pastiche of pastel green
and pink and blue and yellow. Asked the reason for such
coloring, Miz Abernathy only said:

This is a happy house; those are happy colors.

The house was further ringed on all four sides by a

rich-black wrought-iron fence, whose pattern was a corn-husk of the kind, so I'd heard tell, found regularly in the Garden District of New Orleans. Such pattern was a confirmation of the owner's sly and subtle sense of humor, for the rumor was that once there'd been a Mr. Abernathy, able to afford such grand, unseemly opulence, due to being, like our Heyward, a kingpin of the whiskey trade. Twin traits of such a business, the cornerstones, were silence and discretion, and few could find Miz Abernathy short in either.

Her gabled, pastel home drew a very special clientele. No traveling salesmen, no tourists, no families—God forbid—were ever known to stay there, save by error and then but once. Instead, Miz Abernathy's spangled place was home to secret lovers, needing but a drink, some simple food, a place to tryst the night away. No one seemed to know just how this fine tradition first began—Miz Abernathy never made the claim for such intent—but begin it did, and soon her house did flourish as word of its discreet and lively charm spread wide throughout the state and region. All who entered were by silent implication thus protected from outside gossip, rumor. All who entered, simply by their being there, were sworn to hold in silence names of others they might see.

Though rich and famous surely sought such haven, wealth and class were not the keys to entry. The lavish dining room sat twenty-four, twelve tables each for two; upstairs, an even dozen rooms awaited. On any given night, if all within took dinner, one might see by casual glance the governor, a farmer, an out-of-state tycoon, a whiskey transporter, a sheriff. All were served by Miz Abernathy alone, to avoid discomfort that the presence of the kitchen help might bring. Wylie went there often with his tawny

Annalise, and on the night of Wylie's burial, so did I, with sugar Betsy.

We'd been going there for quite some time—the winter places for such trysts were far and few. The first time was a nervous giggle for the both of us, but by the end of number two my sugar Bets had tumbled head and heels in her fondness for the place. She'd come to grow, mature. Hers was quiet beauty, subdued and always wary, that had it not been paired with keen intelligence would easily have stayed austere. Ah, Betsy. Lovely Betsy. For all our many visitations, this place still held her in a slight intimidation. When she and I would find our Fiery Tongue or other, equal, outdoor places for our passion bouts, she was uninhibited, unbound, a part of nature. But on the inside of those pastel-painted shutters, she succumbed to rare Victorian decency. Low lights, she insisted. She undressed beyond my eye, emerging from the large and tiled bath still cloaked in robes, and only when she reached our bed and found the cover of the feather comforter would she recline beside me in all her sugar splendor.

I would kid her about such indoor-outdoor contradiction, but she was firm.

I shrugged, and we would play.

And so we came again to this odd place to enjoy each other in a fond, familiar manner.

We were greeted at the door with smiles and firm condolences. I accepted both. We went upstairs, made love, and bathed, and dressed. We had our dinner, returned once more to our awaiting room, once more made love.

Under such a set of circumstances, the evening was a magic idyll. But quiet Betsy was subdued throughout, and out of sorts.

She left the bed and found her robe and curled into a large, overstuffed chair at the foot of the bed.

I love you, she said.

The flatness in her voice betrayed her keen distemper.

I raised an eyebrow in surprise at such a declaration, said nothing in return. Our lovemaking had been good—always was. I reached for a table at the side of the bed and lit myself a cigarette, poured some whiskey in a plain bathroom glass and offered it to Betsy. She declined, then accepted. Letting the covers fall, I reached to the foot of the bed and handed her the glass. I kissed her hand, returned to lean against the headboard, poured myself an equal glass.

I love you, sugar Betsy said again. I really do love you.

I inhaled, held the smoke until I felt the deep constriction, then released it in a narrow stream in the direction of the vaulted ceiling. I flushed the taste with whiskey swallows that burned my tongue. Still, I said nothing, but stared intently at the beautiful sad dream curled in the chair. I worked my jaw and shrugged, my eyes never leaving hers.

Still, I said nothing.

Do you love me, Andrew?

Why do you ask me?

There was a time when I didn't have to ask, she said, her flat voice now edged with curiosity.

So why do you ask me now? If you want me to say yes, I will. I love you, Betsy Potter.

I smiled sharply, nodded my head imperceptibly.

Andrew, Betsy began in measured lyrics, you have become a son of a bitch to all around you. I love you, but the man I love is not the boy I fell in love with six years ago.

We all change. Six years is a lifetime. A lot of water can tumble over the falls.

But does it take hate to be a honcho big-time race-car driver? she asked.

There was no deflecting her.

It doesn't hurt any, I said.

I've seen you race a lot and heard about some others, she said. What happened between you and Wynn last year never should have happened. You've been friends too long.

That's racing.

That isn't racing, Betsy said, now warming to her task. I can't sit here and tell you how to drive a race car, but I can point out that you are dumping hard on all who ever cared for you.

Who, for chrissakes? Goddamn Wynn and daddy Spencer knock my Wylie out of racing, and I'm supposed to kiss Wynn's silly bloodhound ass?

You still believe the fault of Wylie's crash was theirs?

No, not exactly, no, I said in slight retreat, though even not to her would I call up the real truth.

But they were there, I said again. And wished to be the cause, make no mistake. What is this barroom psychologic hour, anyhow? First One-Eye lays this charge on me —last fall, it was—and now it's you.

You've changed, she said. There's a callous meanness in you far beyond the bumping of a fender here and there. You've withdrawn, even from me—if I may presume to have a slightly special hold on your attention. You've got a chip on your shoulder, but for the life of me I can't obtain the tree from which it came. And neither, I might add, can anybody else of shared acquaintance, yours and mine.

You want out?

If I'd wanted out I would have walked a long time ago, said Betsy. What hurts me most is that we've stopped our

240

sharing. You always were a little quiet. Fine. But the more we're together, the less I sometimes feel I know about you.

I finished my cigarette and lit another from its butt. A thin layer of smoke lay suspended horizontally between us. I poured myself another drink and closed my eyes. I worked to ease the tensing muscles in my face, even as I felt the bilious churning in my stomach. Betsy watched in building silence, left her chair to pour another drink, returned, and curled catlike. I opened my eyes, saw the melancholy pain in hers, and spoke as best I could, in consummation of our Fiery Tongue discussions begun so long ago.

Maybe I'm cursed, I said.

I spoke so softly that Betsy had to strain to hear, with no intended drama.

I am cursed, I said again, with once having believed in the perfectibility of man. Now ask yourself, Miss Betsy Potter, how the sexually indulgent, cigarette-smoking, whiskey-drinking son of a philandering bootlegger could even come to consider such possibility, let alone believe. But I did. When Wylie and One-Eye were off racing, at the first, I'd stay home. And read books. Not a lot of them, mind you—there aren't all that many to be had in Four Corners—but enough for me to find the way to accept the possibility, the *possibility*, mind you, of a man living a perfectly fulfilled life in a perfect world. And what is that, you ask. One in which a man uses his talents to the fullest possible extent, so when he's sixty or seventy or some unimaginable old age, he won't ever have cause to look back and say:

Too bad about that. I never got around to being the best that I could be.

To me, I rambled on, the thought of having to confront such a wasted life was unbearable. The perfect world would be the one in which every single person would be so fulfilled . . . More whiskey, Bets?

She declined, nodding to her glass, half filled. Instead, she took a cigarette, one of six or eight a month that tanned her sugar lips, offered to her with my trembling hand.

I poured myself another two fingers and let the buzzing settle near my weary brain.

So that's what I believed, I continued. Strange, eh? Well, such a noble thought, aided in no little measure by your dear and warming presence, lasted more or less intact, despite much wayward evidence, until the day of Wylie's crash, the one that gimped him—until the day that one whose name I will not call contrived to do him in.

You can't be sure of that, said Betsy. It was an accident. I've seen worse; you've *been* in worse. Just nobody got hurt, is all.

I thought the matter through and told my sugar Betsy of the sabotage, though still I held in silence Uncle Julian's secret role.

The water was there, I said. One-Eye and I found it late that selfsame night. The water didn't get in the gas tank by accident. And then I started thinking of those around me and the others who I'd known. Rex Harding—dead. Wylie—a cripple plagued by ancient demons. One-Eye— if he'd had the guts, he would have sought a greater measure of revenge. Heyward and Dozier—who run the county by corruption, graft. Uncle Julian—a sad, pathetic wonder of a man. Annalise—damn pouty, tawny Annalise.

You forgot Miss Dee.

Hell, she probably gets her Mexican tamales from New Jersey, I said. What really puzzles me—the crux of all my anger and complaint—is that after naming names, a laundry list, I still believe. It disappoints me to the point of a terrible and ferocious anger when I see people who don't live up to what they ought to be. You know who was in the dining room with us tonight?

I couldn't guess, she said. My eyes were only aimed at you.

The junior senator from our great state, for one, with his mistress of long standing. The sheriff of this county, naming two, with the wife of . . . no matter. I'm not perfect —God knows the truth of that—but that doesn't stop me from a terrible anger, which you call hate, when I see things that I do not believe are right. I'm a self-righteous ass and I just can't help myself. Because I don't want to.

Betsy stared, still solemnly austere and glowing, until the ash from her unwavering cigarette fell in silence to the floor. Carefully she bent to pick the ash, still nearly intact, and carried it to the wastebasket. She washed her hands and brushed her teeth. The room was dark, save for a corneal glow from bathroom's way. She took off her robe and hung it on a hook, and wet a washcloth with warm water. She walked to the bed and gently pulled back the covers. She washed my aching balls and withered penis. She took the nearly empty bottle of whiskey and sprinkled my groin. She knelt on the bed at my waist and denied herself the knowledge of the salt-stained tears that trickled down my cheeks, and sucked and sucked and sucked and sucked and sucked.

We had breakfast the next morning in vacant, aching silence and left forever that gay and magic place.

The drive back to Four Corners was short. The false summer had been replaced by low clouds that clung to the rocky-red earth. It began to rain. Crimson rivulets meandered along the side of the road and sometimes crossed it.

Last night, Betsy said, when you listed all the people in your life who'd done wrong things, you didn't mention me.

That's right.

Didn't want to embarrass present company? she asked.

She was relaxed, calm, at ease, purged. Not so I.

No, I said. That wasn't it.

You think I'm perfect? You think *I'm* perfect?

You give great head.

Betsy clasped her hands and jabbed me hard in the ribs. The car swerved, but held the road. We drove in silence to the Stokes County line.

This is the exact place where One-Eye lost his wife, I said. Did you know that?

Not the exact place, I didn't.

We drove to her house and there I stopped the car.

Did last night change your mind about anything? she asked. Anything at all?

No.

Why do you feel you have to be the avenging angel?

I don't know.

No more closer to my sugar Betsy had I ever felt, and no more distant.

CHAPTER
27

Once more the moth wings hover. The chopper waggles side to side. I begin my final ascent.

I am dying. Make no mistake: I am dying, and soon will get to test firsthand the truth of all my philosophic mutterings. The final passage will be quick. This, too, I know with certitude unwavering. The life force flows along a one-way street, declining further mating with my crushed and tarnished body, now strapped and tethered beneath the faint and calming moth wings' beat. I shall not land again on earth alive, but soon will follow, to wherever, Wylie, Mae and Dink and Rex, and all the others of my former knowledge; soon will give my sleek and dapper Jean-Pierre another pause, another name, ungarlanded, to add upon the many he's acquired. Strange, I wish a final conversation with him, for he could tell me much of matters such as this. The spaces widen. I feel no pain; have no desire, such. I cannot decide which damaged part of me has done the fatal blow, but know with overwhelming certainty that I am slipping, slipping, and I have no further urge to fight. My battle's done, for better or for worse; my battle's done, and I am not ashamed. Gently boys, now, gently. I await.

The memories surge. The books are right on this account. The memories surge of all I've done and didn't do and crowd my dimming consciousness for last review. Such perfection that I sought in me and others I surely failed to gain. Nor did they. This thought's an overwhelming sadness, but disattached from shame or fond regret. I can't deny the thought of that which might have been. I'm soon to die in prime of life, so very soon. How will my headstone read? I lay beside the mistress of my unrequited dreams, but cannot learn the shape of what my future might have been. A Circuit rider, bold and true? A Dorsen-sponsored hero? A shark-like whale in the biggest racing pond of all? Or a Wylie–Spencer bullring rider? The mistress of my dreams declines to fill the empty pages of her Andrew Mavis book. Just as well; just as well. They'll have the memory of my dying young to clasp, will not be burdened with the filling of their minds and hearts with memories of a later failure. But, sad to think—there is a wandering regret herein—that down the road a decade, maybe two or three, there'll be no treasure trove of pictures for a younger version of myself to wander through, no yellowed sepia fragments to remind another child, lost, forlorn, of who I was. There'll only be the memories of that which might have been. But memories, on the balance, are a better thing. For unlike tattered, yellow pictures, memories so acquired can't be wounded by the years. Quite the contrary, they gain a new and strong dimension as they twist through warps of time. And so with me.

Hold me close, my sugar Betsy. Hold me close, and once again let's swim and dance in spangled sun of Fiery Tongue. Lather me with charms and quiet kisses while your loves and passions ebb and flow. Ease the furrows in my restless brow. Rub the tensions from my palpitating, sweat-clogged heart. Oil my groin that we might join again and reawaken dormant love. I see the crimson falls and watch you splash away my restlessness. Yes, I loved you—will you ever hear my call?—though I, constricted, could never bring myself to say the words. My sugar Betsy, firm and plump, unyielding in your pursuit to be the outside layer of my conscience, who saw me as I was and chose to turn away from that which I was on the way to being. What future had we, you and I? Hold your memory of the Fiery Tongue. Decline the knowledge of our parting. It is better that we broke apart, especially now. But even in the absence of this terminal conclusion, it is better. Your love for me, though hardly unrequited, was down a narrow alley, wide enough for only one. Hold me close, my sugar Betsy. I would have been a burden.

The black box once again intrudes and clamors for attention—this, the wayward cause, in part, of my condition. What will it show? That much, in my decline, I wish to know. Is it, like me, now shattered on the inside, or will it live to tell, in graphic readout, the whether of our trial, Wynn's and mine? Was that my competition, more than bloodhound Wynn? I'll not go to my grave—soon, now, soon—believing that it played a role in how I acted, what I did. But surely it was one observant passenger. Did I pass its muster?

Or did Wynn? Which one of us had won the gofer's trial? This strikes me as important, this last entanglement of Mavis with a Spencer, though I will never hear the end of it. So long our family lives were mixed, in blood and joy-ride fun, in keen deceit and vengeful retribution. Unfair—unfair's the thought—that he and Spencer never will be told the truth of Wylie's gimping crash, unless, of course, my One-Eye or my Uncle Julian chooses. But they, the Tatums, know the truth, and that will be enough.

Kind and gentle One-Eye, the bedrock floor of all our lives, now soon will see a second Mavis to his rest. Of all I'll miss, he is the one I'll miss the most, if indeed there's any missing to be found within my store. I wonder. Gently boys, now, gently. I wish that I could answer such a call, for I would tell him, gently boys it is. Stoic One-Eye, who in the end chose loyalty to friends, however bad the reciprocity, instead of grief and passionate revenge. He could have folded, years ago, upon the dying of his Mae, did not, but bore ahead. Not indifferent, surely, but surely stoic. He could have raged at Wylie, maybe should have, for Wylie's uncouth violation of his one and only tawny Annalise, but chose to bear their sin, if that is what it was, with dignity and courage. He tutored stubborn bloodhound Wynn, and then to me gave all his knowledge of the race-track art. Was his the life so fully realized that offered benchmark totems for my own? As close as any, now I think, that I will ever know. Surely no one else I've known can offer such a standard. Let One-Eye write my epitaph. There is no other.

The final parting's near. I am weary, so very, very weary. I do not struggle, for a lyric lightness nears my crimson brain and I know the battle's done. My soul, the nether part of me that I've denied so long, blooms lush with flowers from the tattered remnants of my body, and waits. I am near at peace, and now the hovering embrace of raptured light offers balm beyond my richest fantasies. Let go, I tell myself, let go. I must let go and clasp this final mistress to my bosom. The moth wings hum a lighter beat, and far away. Still, I cannot go, not yet, though now I plead with all remaining force to leave this place and find at last my peace. Let me go. It's time. Let me go. And so I cry as ecstasy awaits.

Wylie, O tethered spirit, thrice I denied thee. How many, many times did you deny me? Once . . . to the sky; twice . . . to the sky; three times . . . to the sky. Wylie holds me in his strong and callused hands—one hand alone would be enough, so big is he, so small am I—and tosses me higher, higher to the sky as I scream and giggle with an infant-babe's delight and fear. Higher, higher, he throws me, and when he's done he clasps me to his shoulder. I embrace his bristly neck and chin and smell the rich and fragrant musky odors of the man they call my father. I am the last and final Mavis: no further Mavis seed to grow, not by me or Wylie planted, not in sugar Bets or tawny Annalise. I am the last and final of the demon Mavis clan, a purging that no doubt will be in welcome many places. Tears well up inside my crimson head and trickle down my cheeks and fall to earth. O Wylie, ancient, hoary warrior, I forgive thee. Will you be as kind to me?

What's this? My toes are tingling. And now my feet and legs and groin. And behind the tingling there comes a dull and roaring pain. The two now mix and form a brutal ecstasy, and, intertwining twins, move up my stomach, chest, and neck. And now behind this there's a gentle numbing, creeping slowly, slowly up my body. Once . . . to the sky; twice . . . I can see again. I am whole again, in mind and body. I hear the moth wings beat, softly, softly, and now I watch. The helicopter sways, its deadly cargo slung below, and spirals upward; up, up and away.

Make me my name.